THE PATHOLOGY OF LIES

THE PATHOLOGY
OF LIES

BY JONATHON KEATS

WARNER BOOKS

A Time Warner Company

Warner Books, Inc., 1271 Avenue of the Americas, New York, NY 10020
Visit our Web site at www.warnerbooks.com

W A Time Warner Company

Printed in the United States of America
First Printing: May 1999
10 9 8 7 6 5 4 3 2 1

Library of Congress Cataloging-in-Publication Data

Keats, Jonathon
        The pathology of lies / Jonathon Keats.
            p.   cm.
        ISBN 0-446-67445-1
        I. Title.
        PS3561.E2526P3   1999   98-41168
        813'.54—dc21   CIP

Cover design by Diane Luger
Cover photo by Geoff Spear
Book design by Nancy Sabato

TO MY PARENTS

ACKNOWLEDGMENTS

Itamar Har-Even, Sloan Harris, Jennifer Tucker, Jori Finkel, Fred D'Aguiar, Kate Westerbeck, Matthew Walker, Airié Dekidjiev, Meg Cohen Ragas, Christopher Helman, W. E. Kennick, Sexton Southerland, M.D., Richard Kim, Dale Eastman, Jim Paul, Nicole Müller, Caryl Phillips, Howard Junker

All great men must from their very nature be criminals.

—RASKOLNIKOV

WE MIGHT AS WELL START WITH *Lucrezia Borgia. As legendary for her talent with poisons as for her incestuous relationship with her father, Borgia is a model case. Her name has become synonymous with her art, and her life is now known only in terms of her ability to hasten other people's deaths.*

Catherine de Médicis shared Lucrezia's aptitude for poisons, but her chief contribution to the art was in applying it to matters of state. What for Borgia had been a hobby became a vocation for de Médicis, and within months of her marriage to Henry V of France, undesirables started to vanish. There was the Dauphin François, poisoned with a glass of water between sets of tennis, the wealthy Cardinal of Lorraine, sent from this world with bad money. Hemlock. Foxglove. Aqua toffana. None could match her efforts in the name of religion, though. Just ask the thousands of Huguenots massacred at Catherine's request by her son, Charles IX.

Of course the United States is more democratic than Europe, and so anyone with a taste for pragmatism can succeed. Belle Guinness had nothing but three hundred pounds of her own flesh when she found her calling in life: serial monogamy. Years of hard work netted her a to-this-day uncounted number of dead husbands and a personal fortune of over $50,000, impressive back then. She started by poisoning her children, but spouses proved more profitable, and pretty soon she had a steady flow of them coming to her farm, only to lose their money and their lives. Eventually the farm burned down and nearly a dozen bodies were exhumed. One supposedly belonged to Belle, but few believed it, as she frequently visited town after her funeral. Guinness took her money with her: On the day of the fire, she left only $750 in the bank.

Then there's the legend of Lizzie Borden. Lizzie was a thirty-two-year-old spinster living in her parents' house when she chopped up her father and stepmother with an ax. Lizzie had a number of unfulfilled wishes: (1) electric lighting, (2) an indoor toilet, (3) a piano, and (4) a carriage and chaperone. Lizzie Borden was bored, too. So she took an ax to her father's face during his midafternoon nap, and shattered her stepmother's skull. Lizzie understood the consequences of her actions: She always appeared in court teary-eyed and shrouded. The violent act of parricide, committed by a woman of good upbringing, was unfathomable, and Lizzie knew it. That's what made it brilliant. In recognition of which she was acquitted.

We also learn from history that it's always a mistake to have an accomplice, if only because you cannot trust a killer with your life: Ruth Snyder was in love with a man named Judd Grey. Together they clubbed and chloroformed her husband, then strangled him with picture wire. They tried to cover up the murder by making it look like a burglary gone violent, a story significantly undermined by the discovery of the stolen jewelry under Snyder's mattress. What really ruined it, though, was a coincidence. Snyder's husband was in the habit of keeping a pin with him that had the initials of Jessie Guischard, an old fiancée. JG. The initials matched those of Judd Grey, whose name was listed in Snyder's address book. In questioning, the police asked her a lot of questions, and one was about him. "Has he already confessed?" she asked, shocked and thinking the worst. Both Snyder and Grey were sent to the electric chair.

At least Ruth Snyder's act wasn't frivolous. Had it been successful, she and Grey would have had insurance money and the freedom to pursue each other in bed and out. For truly heinous crimes, you have to look to Jean Harris or Amy Fisher. Emotional trauma is not reason enough to kill, since murdering somebody out of jealousy or pride cannot possibly accomplish anything. It's a stupid risk to take simply for a passing emotion; more important, somebody distraught when killing is not likely to be of the proper mindset to do so effectively. Jean Harris shot Herman Tarnower, the legendary Scarsdale Diet doctor, because he'd left her for a new mistress. Amy Fisher shot Mary Jo Buttafuoco in order to get to her husband. Both acts were pointless, so inevitably both women went to jail. There is nothing empowering about these murders. Acting without good reason, or without sufficient planning, is as inexcusable as getting caught.

G.G.

I. DISSECTION OF THE ANKLE

Make an incision through the integument in the middle line of the leg to the ankle, and continue it along the dorsum of the foot to the toe. Make a second incision transversely across the ankle.

—GRAY'S ANATOMY

THAT CRIMINAL INVESTIGATIONS ARE A nuisance is a self-evident truth, really, to my way of thinking far more self-evident than the truth that all men are created equal. At least that's what I'm trying to explain to my friends Deirdre and Emily, and to myself as well, although there's not much controversy over the point. The difficulty is that we're all rather drunk and I'm having the most troublesome time with my consonants.

This amuses Deirdre no end, and Emily, too, and even I laugh a bit once I've managed to disentangle my tongue from what I'm trying to say. Emily lights a cigarette. Deirdre refills my glass. She pays no attention to what I've been drinking or to whether I've finished yet. "Campari mixes well with *every*thing, Gloria."

I'm prepared to believe her, although it's well known how much she exaggerates. As the token brunette among us, Deirdre's always trying too hard to be outrageous.

Emily, meanwhile, who's somewhat more composed than I, takes control of the conversation. She's off briefly on a tangent about trust-fund managers, and then returns to ask, with her farm-girl smile, whether I'm still screwing the Russian.

I remind her that she asked me the same question last week, that she asks me about my publisher at *Portfolio* every time we're drunk together, and the answer is always the same.

"And what's that?"

"Whenever necessary, and never for recreational purposes." My eyes wander as I say this. I survey the living room for remnants of my cocktail party: glasses everywhere and of every kind imaginable, some I'm certain I don't own. Bits of outerwear remain, too, scarves and the occasional glove left by a drunken guest. People freeze to death in San Francisco in December.

The room returns to focus some seconds later when Deirdre says, "Fucking Dmitri for the good of magazine journalism? How selfless of you. PJ must have trained you well." Her voice is loud and broad, her eyebrows artfully raised above the wire rims of her glasses. Even in my own apartment, Deirdre looks somehow foreign, as if she just stepped out of an Armani ad. People who haven't met her always expect her to speak with an accent. When she doesn't, the temptation is to compliment her on her English.

"Speaking of PJ, isn't it awfully soon to be throwing a party? I mean you *are* a suspect and all."

"I can't stop the planet because of it." I shrug. "Given the direction of things, I doubt I'd have invited him anyway."

Of course, Deirdre's too romantic to understand, and besides, she's busy flipping through my magazines. What she's looking for is me.

"Page fifty-two," I offer, to save her the trouble of going through *Time* cover-to-cover and myself the trauma of having to wait while she does. "They used one of the Klugman photos. A different one."

" 'Gloria Greene Confesses: "I Rather Like the Attention." ' " She reads the caption aloud. This week the FBI hasn't found any evidence for or against me, so I've moved from the news to the entertainment section.

"Lemme see." Emily grabs the magazine away from Deirdre, who glowers at her until she lays it flat on the couch beside me.

"You look fat," Em says triumphantly, filling her cheeks with air. "You should sue."

"She can't," interjects Deirdre. "She a public figure now. They can make her look as fat as they want."

I clear my throat. "I do not look fat, guys." Generally speaking, I'm extraordinarily beautiful, if I do say so myself, at twenty-seven free of wrinkles and other common imperfections. But when the lighting is flat, my face looks bloated rather than round, and my nose all but disappears. A little makeup fixes everything. "Yesterday, Daddy said I remind him of his first Porsche."

Emily and Deirdre just stare at me. Saying nothing.

"He was being obtuse," I explain. "Does anybody know the way to the bathroom?"

"We're in *your* apartment."

"Of course." And then I remember that I've had to pee all night and haven't because it's too much trouble to walk to the bathroom in this state. And I can't face the mirrors everywhere, which never let me lose sight of myself—just when I've managed to escape all the newspapers and magazines and criss-crossed TV signals. That's the merit of alcohol and why the famous always have drinks in their hands at parties. "Somebody pour me more. Please."

A new drink finds its way to my hands, this one light and icy. I hold it up. "To our deaths!"

"To our deaths!" they repeat in unison.

We drink and Deirdre asks Emily about the ad campaign she's working on. Vici Sport. She's an account exec at Taylor Knight, one of their best, apparently, or so she's told us. Vici is her latest coup, accomplished by offering athletes big endorsement money without company permission. She's never worn sneakers a day in her life, doesn't ever plan to, either, and now she's got all these new shoes she's perpetually trying to pawn off on others. She's already given me three pairs, one for tennis, one for running, and one for pentathlons, whatever those are. I've in turn tried to give them to people at the office, but of course they all have different shoe sizes and most of them exercise as little as I do. People always mistake me for a tennis player and a swimmer and a skier. The last time I was in Aspen was when I was seventeen and with Daddy. The last time I was in a pool was when I was twelve. I've never played tennis.

"Product sell-through . . . brand imaging . . . cross-training poodles . . ." Emily's still talking because Deirdre's in human resources and never has anything interesting to say. They've lit cigarettes. I've got one, too. As far as I recall, I don't smoke. My glass is sticky and my mouth tastes of peppermint. I try to ask a question, to find the conversation, but lose my place before words reach my tongue. Deirdre is sorting through the clothing left behind, pocketing a scarf that appeals to her and offering another to Emily.

Emily shakes her head. "You shouldn't steal, Deir. You might get Gloria in trouble."

PORTFOLIO IS LOCATED ON A SINGLE floor of a former warehouse in San Francisco's South of Market district. Given the magazine's size, space is at a premium. Our offices are generally as crowded as Dickens novels, cubicles as cramped as the stories of Henry James. Of course, there are exceptions. Mine is one, Dmitri's another. But no office comes even close in square footage to the colossal conference room.

Dmitri, founder, owner, publisher of *Portfolio,* is something of a collector. His own space is cluttered with a hopeless jumble of flavorless Victoriana and tasteless Americana perpetually in danger of being upset by his enormous heft. The conference room was, too, once, although now it's as it was when I started at *Portfolio*: bare except for a sixteen-foot-long mission oak table and twenty-odd matching chairs. The effect is humbling. This is a place where business gets done.

Today the business has to do with the fact that PJ's dead.

Not that this is late-breaking news: My staff has known the truth for weeks. It's the reason PJ no longer works at *Portfolio,* and that I'm a suspect. It's the reason I'm now editor-in-chief.

◆　◆　◆

Prior to PJ's death, I was food editor at *Portfolio.* Dmitri thinks I'm a gourmet chef.

Dmitri thinks a lot of things about me, most of them untrue. That's why, at the age of twenty-four, with no prior professional experience as an editor and a knowledge of cooking food no greater than you'd expect of somebody with my upbringing, I was selected over considerable competition to run the restaurant section.

I'd initially been taken on as an unpaid intern, one of three in the editorial department. It was my first job out of college. My mother didn't consider it a job at all. Daddy fortunately disagreed with her, understanding the value of experience as only he could. He paid my salary. He gave me $36,000 and somehow managed to keep me on his health insurance policy. It was generous of him. More generous, in fact, than PJ could be when finally he offered me a paid position.

I became food editor largely by coincidence. By the time the position opened, I'd have applied for almost anything at the magazine. Internships generally last one year. I had been there eleven months.

The day that the previous food editor, an old warhorse who'd survived botulism and gout, announced his retirement, I slipped off to the Civic Center library. I'd never spoken more than a mouthful of words to him, and had never spent much time looking at his section, and so wasn't at all sure what he did or why. I checked out every book I could find on food, from the *Larousse Gastronomique* to Brillat-Savarin's *Physiology of Taste.* For good measure, I also checked out a volume of Dorothy Parker's early book reviews. Parker was a hero of mine. I was even briefly tempted to sign my reviews "Constant Eater."

My head full of fruit compote and fois gras, I went to PJ the next morning. PJ liked me. He liked the fact, he later told me, that I always wore wool sweaters and loose-cut blazers and that I was so serious all the time. He was thirty-nine. He had a case of psoriasis and he'd absently pick at the rough skin behind his ears with the temple of his eyeglasses, flaking it onto his dark, expensive clothing until it appeared he was growing lichens. Obviously he wanted to fuck me.

PJ: Do you know anything about food?
GLORIA: I know *every*thing about food.

PJ smiled. This is what he liked best about me.

And so, against the wishes of Jake, our managing editor, and without Dmitri's knowledge, I was granted a formal interview. The former food editor refused to get involved, busy as he was on a book about botulism and gout and how he'd survived both, and PJ knew even less about food than I did. Résumés had piled up, and he'd interviewed countless others before picking me. PJ was my savior.

People wander into the conference room, trading seats for gossip. In all, there are twenty-four of us, a tangle of editors, designers, and salespeople who get along about as well as one might expect, given the combination of egos and ids inherent in such a group. The stress of being at the center of a major criminal investigation probably hasn't helped matters, but it does make life less dull.

Portfolio is a large magazine, or at least as large as a magazine can be without sacrificing its own literacy. We're not *The Saturday Evening Post,* and we don't care about our readers' opinions. They appreciate that. As a rule, readers have no editorial instinct and so seldom know what they want. Ours are the young, the urban, the professional, and about the only thing that doesn't interest them is young urban professionalism. It's a matter of preying on their insecurity and feeding their imagination with stories of the tragically hip. None of the staff that matters is from San Francisco or even California, and so we understand things one generally doesn't on the West Coast. Loaded with snide celebrity profiles, fortified with unverifiable society gossip, spiked with a vocabulary at once too sophisticated and too vulgar for Merriam-Webster, *Portfolio* is a sort of pornography. As important as facts may be, what matters in the end is attitude.

I call the meeting to order and announce that, in light of PJ's death, we're to run a lengthy obituary in the upcoming issue. "What this means," I explain, "is that we'll need to cut a page." I ask Jake what our letters section looks like.

He slurps the last of the jelly from his otherwise uneaten donut and says it's pretty full.

"Anything interesting?"

"Just the usual cranks."

"And how will this effect production?" This is a question for Adam, the stringbean-shaped art director.

"It can't be done."

"Yes it can."

Adam stares at me through his lensless Buddy Holly

glasses. He shrugs. "It'll screw things royally." His two assistants nod until he motions to them to stop. "When can you have the text to me?"

"I can write it in under an hour," Jake says, hands massaging the soft hull of his donut, coercing from it whatever grape residue remains.

I tell him that will be unnecessary.

"What do you mean, unnecessary?"

"You're not writing the obit."

"Then who is?"

"I'm writing the obituary. This is public relations, Jake. Do you really think the public wants to associate *Portfolio* with someone like . . . you?" I smile. "When I need you to do something, I'll tell you."

"I'm sick of this bullshit," Jake mutters through sugar-encrusted fingers. "You're a fucking suspect. Doesn't anybody remember that?"

"Nobody takes it seriously, Jake. Nobody except you. You'd think I'd done something wrong."

◆　◆　◆

Because Jake thinks of himself as a journalist, he despises ambiguity on principle. But murder is a messy thing. Even PJ's body wasn't found all at once. In fact, due to a shipping error on the part of UPS, it's still not fully recovered. Part of one leg remains at large.

It took several days even to learn that PJ was past-tense. At first it was just a disappearance. Then some time passed and Myra, the marketing manager, got a call from one of her list suppliers. Seems they'd received what they took to be a strikingly lifelike mock forearm, severed and blood-encrusted and smelling of rot. They knew it had come from our office because it was one of their mailing labels on the package, a label with a code Myra had ordered. They'd seeded the list they'd sold us, as list sellers will, included their own company name to ensure that we didn't use it for an unauthorized or inappropriate mailing, and what they'd gotten back was a very real-looking body part in a state of modest decay. This wasn't the sort of promotion they'd had in mind when they licensed the list to *Portfolio*. Needless to say, they weren't pleased.

Myra insisted she'd not even sent her lists to the mailhouse yet, and were they sure it was shipped by *Portfolio*? They read her the code. She found the list. Several labels were missing, among them one in the list vendor's Zip code. Somebody, or perhaps everybody, called the police.

The forearm was real, it turned out, and it explained a few other calls to police around the country. Body parts were dropping everywhere, it seemed, blistered, putrefied, in varying states of decomposition.

Of course the FBI got involved, once it became clear that severed body parts were crossing state lines, which threw Dmitri in a panic. Dmitri lived in Leningrad for the first thirty years of his life, and for ten published an underground anti-Communist newspaper. If there was one thing the experience taught him, it was to avoid interaction with men in dark suits.

Which is why he put me in charge when PJ's severed head was recovered in L.A., and I offered to handle the public: "Good idea. You knew PJ the best. I *trust* you, Gloria."

Then there was the trip down south, the positive identification of PJ, the press conference, my first ever, and the start of the formal investigation. I returned to San Francisco early the next morning. When I saw my picture on page one of the *Chronicle,* I knew I'd found what was always lacking in my life. I'd discovered what was important, and I only had to pursue it.

A few days later I persuaded Dmitri to give me PJ's old title so as to prevent confusion within the media and insubordination at the magazine. Because PJ's office was still taped off, crisscrossed with yellow plastic ribbon like a Mardi Gras parade, I had to set up temporarily in the conference room. I gave the investigators my old office in which to question and fingerprint the staff, and had Spivvy serve coffee at regular intervals. The investigators liked me. They appreciated my attentiveness and eagerness to cooperate.

Still, it was only natural that I be made a suspect. People at the magazine talked, and soon it was clear to the investigators and my fellow journalists all over the country that I had a motive, intimate access to PJ, and a certain talent. The only thing lacking was concrete evidence.

THREE

WITH MURDER IN THE PAPERS, THE phones at *Portfolio* ring without pause. Honestly, I think I'm going deaf in my right ear.

A single trip to the women's room nets a message from my father, one from Agent Brody of the FBI, and a callback from Gordon Williston, the professional unauthorized biographer I've assigned a story on the L.A. debutante scene. *Just infiltrated the Junior League. Please advise how to proceed.*

I can't deal with the others, so I dial my reporter. Gordy's telephone number is eleven digits long. By the time I've punched the first three, reception pages: "Some policeman on line five. He won't give his name."

"They never do, Spivvy." They never do and they're all oblivious to the fact that I've no time in my life for new people. The last thing I need is another interrogation. "Tell him I'm out robbing a bank."

"And the woman at *Newsweek* called again. Should I con-nect—"

I hang up in the middle of Gordy's number and tell Spivvy I'll call her myself. *Newsweek* often knows more about my case than I do.

She picks up on the first ring. *"Fernandez,"* she says, as jour-nalists who fancy themselves serious are prone to do.

"It's Gloria."

"Nobody's talking to me. I called Agent Brody earlier, and they referred me to the press officer in D.C. Brody *never* does this when I'm—"

"He's just more interested in me than in you."

"Seriously, Gloria, I'm on deadline. Do you have an update on PJ?"

"Still dead."

"That's not what . . ." She sighs. "You wouldn't want an issue to pass without your name in print, would you?"

"Profile me again. Everybody else has."

"Do you have a confession to make?"

"I'm sure I could fabricate one. In return for a cover shot."

"Thanks, but I think I'll settle for a quote."

"Hold on." I look down a list of lines I've prepared for this purpose, each with a checkbox next to it so I don't repeat my-self and become a bore. "How's this: 'The FBI should be glad PJ's dead. An editor of his caliber would kill for the opportu-nity to expose such slovenly work. This is an open invitation to professional criminals everywhere. These days, America really is the land of the free.'"

". . . 'professional criminals.'" In the background I hear the tapdance of fingers turning my words to ink. "Or 'professional murderesses'?"

"As you prefer. You're the reporter."

And then it's Spivvy interrupting again. "Dr. Greene on line two—"

"Daddy!" I disconnect Fernandez.

"You don't know what you're missing, princess, editing that magazine all day long."

"Just finish lifting another face, did we?" Part of what makes Daddy a brilliant doctor is that he never knows how a body modification will look before he starts cutting. Like a boy with a chemistry set.

"Tucking a tummy, actually. There were the most fascinating complications."

"Tell me."

"You'll join me for dinner, then? I still have reservations at Etruscan."

"I already explained."

"You have a date."

"Nothing serious. A writer. I need a favor from him."

"You're dating a writer."

"He's married. Children. On Prozac. Named Perry. I don't think you need to worry, Daddy." My father is always doing this. Protecting me from the elements. Protecting me from myself.

"You know where to reach me."

"I love you, Daddy. More than anybody. But I have a call on line—"

Agent Brody. The FBI intimidates Spivvy, so she tends to ring them through without asking my permission.

"I've just been telling *Newsweek* the most flattering things about you."

"You always amaze me, Gloria."

"Thank you."

"But I never had a chance to compliment you on your candor in last week's issue of *Time.*"

"Isn't it the most godawful photo? Positively criminal."

"But a flattering story, once again. The quote from your high-school English teacher. And your father."

"He has to be nice to me. I'm his only daughter."

"And his best student."

"Everything important I learned from him."

"He's quite a doctor, isn't he?"

"Do you need some liposuction?"

"Quite a surgeon."

"He used to practice on burn victims."

"At UC San Francisco."

"He was the best they had."

"Where he was also an instructor."

"Only the most talented are."

"An instructor in human anatomy. Dissection, if I'm not mistaken. His students always had the best corpses."

"Yes. In his class, PJ would never have made the grade. I doubt I would have, myself."

FOUR

THE FIRST THING TO UNDERSTAND about cadavers is that they're soaked in formaldehyde for several years before they're dissected. As a result, they're useful from an anatomical standpoint, but preserve none of the textures or consistencies of a living body. The skin becomes as dry as writing paper. The muscles change, too, turning tough and stringy, like turkey cooked too long. Most dramatic of all is the metamorphosis of the brain: *in vivo* it's a wet, gelatinous mass; in the cadaver it's as tight as a Superball. Cadavers are bloodless. Colorful bits of string mark the points at which veins have been spliced for draining, arteries for formaldehyde injection. Formaldehyde smells of gin. Cheap gin on the breath after a night of heavy drinking.

It's unusual, I know, but when I was twelve, I learned human anatomy from Daddy. We worked in the evenings when the medical school was quiet. Daddy had an extra cadaver set aside, and it was on that body that we worked. I was required to read the textbook before performing any dissections, and I was also expected to take all the tests. Daddy secretly scored me against his students. Mostly I was ahead of the curve.

Before it belonged to me, my cadaver belonged to an eighty-three-year-old brain hemorrhage victim. He was tall and skinless and had a large, heavy penis like a totem pole with its narrative washed away. His fingers felt of old paint. Daddy wouldn't permit me to name the cadaver. He said you can never name a cadaver because then it becomes human, which is always too messy to deal with when what matters is the position of your scalpel, the accuracy of your incision. Even when he operated on women he saw socially, added to or subtracted from their flesh according to the prevailing fashions, he'd developed the discipline to forget their voices and their marital histories and their favorite drinks. With the help of his anesthesiologist, he could reduce them to mere slabs of muscle, fat, bone: sculptor's supplies to be manipulated, brought to life. Daddy didn't let me name my cadaver because he wanted me to learn what he knew. To be like him.

What mattered to Daddy was ritual. We always wore scrubs and surgical gloves, and I tied my hair back. Daddy had a wooden stepladder he'd borrowed from the library for me that I'd stand on so I'd be tall enough to work. Before touching scalpel to cadaver, we'd discuss what we wanted to see and how we expected to locate it. If I was right, he'd reward me with a dry kiss to the lips.

Bodies are irregular things. Nerves, tendons, even major arteries aren't always where you'd expect them to be. Textbooks can only approximate the anatomy of any given cadaver. This is part of the challenge of dissection, and one of its lessons. Science may be all numbers and equations, but medicine is an art.

Dissecting a cadaver is not unlike editing an article: In both you must find the essential in what is often a large and unwieldy mass.

Daddy let me do most of the work with the scalpel, but certain aspects of the dissection required his help. What they say about dead weight is true; Daddy was accustomed to the strain. Few men and fewer women understand that intellect is as physical as it is mental, and if you can't enact your ideas, you might as well give up thinking altogether. With Daddy, I could leverage my intelligence. When I pretended to be him, I could move bodies, too.

Daddy was still more or less married to my mother then, and she was not altogether enthusiastic about my supplementary education. I think she was jealous that we spent so much time together, and that our activities necessarily excluded her. Sometimes we took three hours a night. Eventually she said two sessions a week was the most she'd tolerate. Even that much, she wasn't sure was healthy.

At school my teachers liked me for the most part, despite the fact that, or perhaps because, I wasn't so popular with the student body. I was the one who'd always do the homework and the extra credit and was able to answer the tough questions. I'd never been able to win an elected seat in student government or successfully audition for a student play, and nobody understood me when I was honest and what new friendships I scavenged never lasted the semester, but at least I could take comfort in my unusual brilliance. At the time I wanted to be everything, and all at once, so genius would help. I promised myself I'd remain humble.

Which is why Mr. Pope's frustration with my behavior in biology class so devastated me. When he asked one day, in that plush, carpeted voice of his, to speak to me after school, I felt certain it was to compliment me on my command of the inner ear. Instead he took me into his office to remind me that *he* was the one teaching the class, and that, while my participation was valued, I should limit myself to occasional brief, relevant comments. "Try to be more like your classmates," he urged me, and then his face went blurry behind my tears and all I could see was the wallet-brown mole on his cheek.

I cried again that evening, for Daddy, and he threatened to call the headmaster. He said I was too advanced, that was the trouble, and Mr. Archbishop, or whatever the fuck his name was, probably just felt threatened. He said what I was thinking before even I could articulate it.

Daddy understood me. I am not an easy person to understand.

FIVE

"**S**o did you or didn't you?" Deirdre asks, getting right to the point.

She is sitting across from me at Gio's, a bistro just off Union Square, leafing through her Caesar salad for croutons. Although we've been here a thousand times before and she knows what to expect of the Caesar salads, she's been whining the whole meal through that her dressing is too strong.

If only to shut her up, to keep her from complaining throughout lunch and for the rest of our lives, I've agreed to tell her how my date with Perry Nash went. I've agreed to answer anything she wants to ask.

"Well, did you or didn't you?"

"Sort of, I guess."

"What do you mean, *sort of*?" She bites into another crouton. "Either you did or you didn't. Unless, that is, there were . . . potency issues."

I lean toward her, taking care not to put my elbow into my bread dish. "What I mean is that he did me from behind."

"From *what*?"

I repeat to Deirdre what I've said. I tell her that I let the guy do me from behind.

"You don't mean in the style of *le chien*, do you? You mean from—"

"Don't act shocked. It's not like I'm so fucking conservative. Besides, it wasn't intentional."

"What do you mean?"

What I'm trying to say is that the whole thing was weird, that I generally don't go out with writers anymore unless I'm desperate for an article. I'd figured on first base, maybe second if Perry promised to meet deadline and write it the way I wanted him to. Nothing irresponsible; just another way to compensate him for his services. We're all endowed with certain assets, or at least the most fortunate of us are, and anyone who lets them go to waste doesn't deserve to succeed. I appreciate the advantages I've been given, and if the object of my desire is handsome like Daddy, I sometimes even find enjoyment.

But to go into all this with Deirdre seems too daunting. I've not had enough to drink. Besides, Deirdre always needs everything explained to her three times if she's to be satisfied. She claims it's because she's dumb, but I know her too well. She does it to check for consistency.

"I didn't mean for it to turn out that way, both of us naked and him checking his fucking pager all the time, afraid his wife might worry. You can't prepare for these things."

"I do," Deirdre enunciates. "You have to be careful, Glor. Psychopaths are everywhere these days. He could hurt you."

"Nobody can hurt me."

"I mean physically." She frowns. "Did he have good bedside manner?"

"He was simply awful. Kept interrupting the sex to say he was falling in love with me. I mean, it's one thing to humor a guy you don't really like, but quite another to hear him babble about eternity while he rubs your Oil of Olay on his penis. Finally I told him to shut up or leave."

"You are so cold, Glor. Does he have kids?"

"He showed me pictures."

"Tell me what it was like."

"It's like when anyone shows you pictures of children, especially their own. You make vacuous comments, use words like *photogenic* a lot."

"That's not what I'm talking about, Gloria. What was *it* like?"

"You mean you've never done it like that before?"

"Have you?"

"No."

"What was it like?"

I look at the tables around us. An elderly couple, deeply submerged in the task of eating soup, to our left. The people to our right just gone, their tablecloth ruffled like an unmade bed.

"It was another body. Hardly matters whose or what point of contact is involved. The physical thrill is unavoidable, even if it is uncomfortable. It's about invasion. You know that." But she's staring at me, wrinkly-nosed.

"And love?"

"Invasion, Deir. You can't separate the physical and the emotional. I keep explaining that to you. Somebody gets conquered, creamed. Like you do every month."

"You've never been—"

"Bullshit. Some relationships are harder to understand."

"I feel sorry for Perry."

"I'll admit it's a little cynical. But the transaction was legitimate. All the numbers added up."

Shaking her head and muttering about prostitution, Deirdre leaves me for the women's room. As usual I pay no attention to her criticism, and then the check arrives. It's my turn to pay. Aside from the half-dozen croutons, Deirdre hasn't eaten any of her salad. I've only started my arugula.

The busboy clears our plates. The waiter takes the check and Deirdre reappears, lips smeared a bloodier shade of red. She seats herself, returns her napkin to her lap. We stare at each other.

"You going to jail anytime soon?" she asks.

The joke has grown old, but still it amuses her. I think she derives a perverse pleasure from seeing my name used to sell newspapers. Nobody worthwhile takes my suspect status seriously, even those who officially should. Particularly because I'm a woman. How could I possibly have overpowered PJ? But, what with the dismemberment and his prominence in the magazine community, the column inches keep pouring in, like love letters from a flustered suitor. The recognition is pleasant enough, although the investigation does grow tiresome. People sometimes say nasty things, as if I'd not earned my position on the masthead. PJ is dead; long live *Portfolio.*

"Have they at least located PJ's upper leg?"

"Still AWOL."

"Maybe you didn't package it properly." She grins.

"I don't see why it matters, Deirdre. At this point it's useless anyway."

The smile wavers. "Have you seen an attorney yet? The one Emily recommended?"

"Whatever for? Was there something in the *Examiner* today I missed? Have I been arrested without being told?" I check my wrists, but there are no handcuffs.

"We're just trying to help. An attorney might *prevent* your arrest. You act like Brody and Emmett are closer friends than Emily and me."

"You two are irreplaceable. Nobody will arrest me."

"What happened to my salad?" she says.

"The waiter took it. You were in the bathroom."

Deirdre frowns again, touches fingers to lips. I run my purse strap over my shoulder. She drains the last of her wine and then reaches across the table for my glass.

SIX

THE CONFERENCE ROOM ALWAYS FEELS empty when just the editors meet, and even more so since Jake resigned. Currently there are seven of us around the mission oak table. Seven of us and acres of empty chairs.

Ungraceful as Jake could be, he was effective at his job. Editors as a group are even touchier than writers about their value. Add to that issues of territory, and you'll have some idea of the complexity of managing those who perceive themselves as both talent and scout. Jake knew his staff well, and despite the grumbling around the office about his refusal to shower daily and his habit of leaving crumbs of whatever he happened to be eating wherever he happened to be eating it, he was respected for his competence.

It's a shame he had to go. A shame he had to bring up all those unwelcome questions with answers that could benefit nobody.

Bruce is a different story. As former computer systems manager, he knows his way around the office without Spivvy's help, but to him the magazine has never been more than a series of server files and backup tapes. Bruce is pleasant enough; he doesn't drink on the job, insists on holding the door for those who are female or over sixty. He's shorter than I am by at least three inches, and I'm under five-eight. Really, I see him as a role model for the editors. The greatest risk in a transition is that the staff will resist a new vision without grasping its merits. I don't expect my staff to understand me. *Portfolio* isn't produced for their entertainment. My obligation is to the public; my staff's obligation is to its editor-in-chief. Unlike Jake, Bruce knows his place. For the greater good of *Portfolio,* I have made him my assistant. I have promoted Bruce to managing editor.

We're currently at work on the February issue, which goes to press in under two weeks. The January issue just hit the newsstands. It's December 22. Because of the ordeal with the obituary, it came out three days late.

Bruce has little to say when I ask him for his first weekly update. He sucks at the tip of his ballpoint pen until ink streaks his lips, then announces that the cover story has gone back to the writer for final edits. I'm perfectly aware it was sent back; I'm the one who sent it.

"So, no news on the wisdom industry exposé?" I look down at my runsheet as I say this. The changes are a blur, a fine filigree of handwriting overtaking the type like a layer of soot. Nobody has bothered to issue an update in over a week. I push my reading glasses up the bridge of my nose and ask Bruce when he plans to provide one.

"I'm still not sure the wisdom industry fits our—"

"Never mind wisdom. Runsheets, Bruce. Stick to what you

understand. Katherine, where do we stand on reviews?" Katherine is our book section editor, and long ago gave up on human interaction.

She glances briefly at me, then returns to cleaning her glasses. She licks each lens, as if no one were looking, methodically working her tongue from the center to the edges. Don Richard, the fashion editor, watches with fascinated repulsion as she soaks up the saliva on her silk blouse.

"Three book reviews are in," she says when she's through, "but two aren't acceptable. I wish you wouldn't make assignments in my section without asking first. I like Dostoevsky too, but that doesn't mean we should review his novels in 'Word of Mouth.'"

"That wasn't a review I commissioned. It was an *appreciation*. To put his work in context."

"But having Charles Manson write it?" She frowns. "What if he doesn't like my line-edits?"

"Excuse me?" interrupts Moira, who edits technology, always in longhand, usually in purple. "We have a world-famous murderer writing for us?"

"Two. If PJ's obit counts as writing." Chiming in now is Dan, night-life editor, navy watchcap, orange parka-vest, Greenwich Village sneer.

"This is not open for discussion," I remind my staff. "Nobody here is commissioning challenging stories, and if *I'm* sick of reading this magazine, you can imagine how our readers feel."

"Under PJ—"

"PJ doesn't work here anymore. I'll not repeat his mistakes out of reverence or laziness. You have to trust my vision now. I'm sorry that Charles Manson offends your literary sensibilities, Katherine, and that I offend yours, Dan, but from this point on, that's how we're going to operate."

"But Dmitri—"

"Dmitri isn't your concern, either. I am. Stay or leave, I honestly don't care. A successful magazine reflects its editor and anticipates its time. I'm not after megalomania here. What I'm after is making a legendary publication of a third-rate knock-off *Vanity Fair.*" I smile. "Now, Rake will tell us which major music celebrity will be suing us for libel next month."

When Rake, our tone-deaf music editor, starts stroking his chin stubble and listing singers whose names mean nothing and whose sexual habits mean even less, Don Richard nudges Katherine. He taps her shoulder with his pinkie and she tries to shrug it off, but Don keeps poking until she scoots her chair around and says, "What?"

"Nothing."

"What is it, Don?"

"It's not important." He frowns. "Yes it is. Do you have any mousse? My hair . . ." He points to his head, blond and spiky like a lint brush.

Katherine shakes her head, pulling her fat purse to her body. "Not until you return my hand cream and my eye liner." Don Richard has stolen cosmetics from all of us. Whenever I'm missing something, the first place I look is in his desk drawer. "Ask Gloria for mousse. Ask Dan."

Katherine returns her attention to Rake. Don Richard reaches into her bag and palms a hairbrush.

". . . which is a real problem we're facing, Gloria. I mean, we *could* smuggle some junk into detox for her. The interviewer has done that for vocalists before. The question is, will she agree to shoot up with him in the room? Now that she's been born again . . ."

I've no idea who we're talking about or why, and it occurs to me that the reason is that it's time for lunch.

"This meeting is adjourned," I announce.

"We haven't discussed—" Dan again. The night life in San Francisco is too dull ever to change meaningfully, so there's hardly any reason to bring up his section in meetings. We've not done so since I started.

"Adjourned, Dan. Go buy yourself a sandwich."

I gather my papers. Dan and Katherine grumble to each other, and to Moira, too. Rake and I are the last ones to leave the conference room. He follows me into the hallway. His after-shave smells spicy, like pumpkin pie.

"Dan doesn't know better," he offers.

"Dan?"

"All those rumors. I don't know how you handle them. Like that piece in *The National Enquirer.*"

"*Enquirer?*"

"Page one. Don't you ever buy groceries?"

"Express lane." When Rake doesn't continue, I prompt, "What did it say?"

"They had photos. They claimed your dissection was textbook-perfect except for—"

"The oblique fracture to the clavicle. Happens all the time, Rake. People walk around for years and don't know it."

"Um, no . . . Except that the heart was torn free and partially digested."

"That's *disgusting.* Do I honestly look like a cannibal?" I pull my hair away from my face.

But Rake's not smiling. He's just staring as if I had a spot on my blouse. A knife in my palm. *"Oblique fracture to the clavicle?"*

SEVEN

I READ THE BULK OF MY MAIL ON THE stairway to my apartment, feeling my way forward with the tips of my pumps. I don't correspond often, but I get many Christmas cards in big red envelopes. Mostly they come from old boyfriends, some now living abroad, and say the same sort of things and are interesting only for their postmarks: *Wish you were here. Is it true what they said about you in* The Economist *last week? I always knew you'd make a killing.*

In my apartment, I drop my briefcase and pour myself a glass of wine. It's a nonvintage Chardonnay that tastes of old clothing. A gift from PJ. Congratulating me for something spectacular, no doubt.

I unbutton my coat and let it slide to the floor. I wander my kitchen, impatiently flipping through cabinets, peering into drawers. I set a pot of water to boil.

I alphabetize the Christmas cards atop my refrigerator by last name of sender, and then I throw away those from people who I think are no longer in love with me. Tomorrow is Christmas Eve. Already the whole planet is on vacation: the magazine closed through the weekend, Agents Brody and Emmett home for the holidays helping their mothers mash potatoes and carve the roast. I'm exhausted. To boil a pot of water takes all my concentration.

This happens to me sometimes, and more often now. I've learned to stay home. I've learned not to answer the phone or the door. When morning comes, I tell people I was out having a reckless time. I don't mention the hundreds of books read, pages pinned beneath salt bowl and pepper mill, over pasta and Chianti. It's bad enough to be a woman and an editor; education is acceptable only to a point.

Nobody ever taught me the finer points of femininity, and for this reason other women fascinate me: the habit of phrasing every answer as if it were a potential question, every question as if it were a potential insult, and every insult as if it were a potential apology. People don't let me play games with them because they know I want to win and that's against the rules unless I'm cheating and everybody's aware, in which case it's endearing. Women fascinate me, but men are the only ones who ever let me forget that, by all standards, I'm fucked up. If only it were my politics. But I don't have politics; all I have is me and all I know are my own desires, for this little black dress and for that magazine editorship. I'm not afraid to pursue my ambitions. My words are everywhere, because that's what it means to be a woman under investigation for murder. My words and my image reminding me that I'm an exception. For Emily and Deirdre, it's entertainment. For the FBI, it's evidence. For Daddy, it's a perverse form of immortality. And for me, it's maybe the origin of a new identity.

Tonight I cook capellini in pesto. While the pasta boils, I open my refrigerator, a small space packed with alcohol and the foods I crave: chevre, cornichons, maraschino cherries. In the freezer I keep vodka and ice. Deirdre recently brought over a pint of mocha fudge frozen yogurt we somehow never ate. I take it from its shelf. I peel back the lid and graze the surface with a tablespoon.

I shut off the stove. The pasta sinks, half-cooked. Wasted.

In bed, I scoop frozen yogurt into my mouth. I open a novel. I'm rereading *Crime and Punishment* because everybody says I could learn from it.

I wear all my clothes to bed. I've brought my Chardonnay with me, and with it the bottle. My sheets grow warm against my silk blouse, my stocking feet.

It is just past nine o'clock. I've only heard the phone ring once. Daddy was calling for me. He couldn't wait for tomorrow night. He left a message. He called to ask me on a date.

II. DISSECTION OF THE KNEE

Make a vertical incision along the middle of the back of the thigh, from the lower fold of the nates to about three inches below the back of the knee-joint, and there connect it with a transverse incision, carried from the inner to the outer side of the leg. Make a third incision transversely at the juncture of the middle with the lower third of the thigh.

—GRAY'S ANATOMY

ONE

THIS YEAR THE STUARTS SERVE WASSAIL from an enormous carnival glass punch bowl into green carnival glass cups. Daddy's wearing Armani. I'm wearing Valentino. People compliment us on what a spectacular couple we make.

Christmas Eve at the Stuarts is an affair of Fitzgeraldean proportions. Mr. Stuart wears a burgundy velvet tuxedo with lapels as wide as Zelda's mood swings, and Mrs. Stuart's dress matches the living room curtains just so. The Stuarts live in San Francisco, on Broadway. Their house is not larger than those surrounding it, but somehow it matters more. Like most of San Francisco worth mentioning, it was built just after the earthquake. The Stuarts had already lived in San Francisco for three generations.

"You must be Gloria Greene," Brian Edward Reed-Arnold announces while Daddy replenishes my cup. Brian is one of the endless Stuart nephews, mid-twenties, attractive in an America's Cup kind of way. The sort of person who's as easy to talk to as he is to forget. "I've read *all* about you."

"We've never met."

"You're beautiful."

"I am. Thank you."

"I work in mergers and acquisitions."

"How eighties." I smile at him. "Have you merged or acquired anything interesting lately?"

"There was *The Algonquin* . . ." Of course *The Algonquin* is the most legendary magazine in the country, maybe the world, known for its 25,000-word stories on poets, botanists, and zinc. It hasn't been profitable in decades.

"Art Reingold bought that over three years ago. I hope you've done business since."

"I have. Most recently—"

"Have they filled the editorship at *The Algonquin* yet? Art should hire me, really."

"The cultural aristocracy meets the criminal element."

"Criminal element?"

"I thought you'd promised to confess. If the media coverage was good enough."

"That was a fucking misquote. *Newsweek* lacks all sense of irony."

"On the news they said an arrest was imminent. Are you in hiding here?"

"Hiding? Everybody knows I've nothing to hide, and least of all myself. I'm famous."

When Daddy sees me getting ruffled, he puts his arm around my waist. I introduce him to Brian, smiling, handsome.

"What sort of medicine do you practice, Dr. Greene?"

"Reconstructive surgery."

"Cosmetic surgery," I correct.

Daddy glares. Says nothing.

"It's why all the women here look alike." I gesture broadly. "It's why they all look like me."

Daddy uses me as his model when he rebuilds others' faces. High cheeks, thin lips, and rounded features have in the past decade become suspiciously common among the ageless Stuart set. My nose, straight, short, and turned up to make me look perpetually conceited, has also made the rounds.

"So you're Gloria's husband," Brian says.

"Daddy's my father." I giggle. "Same concept."

"Excuse me?"

"We're madly in love." I peck Daddy on the cheek, and then I dodge them both.

Others find me. Soon there's a crowd and I'm making up stories about my life in crime.

"Mostly what comes up with the FBI are issues of protocol. If I'm to be interrogated, I certainly don't want to do it in a stuffy office. So I ask if we can go out for coffee, or rather tea. One of the agents has an allergy to coffee beans."

"Have you been to Tea Incorporated in the Fillmore?" Bilkie, who's five months pregnant and in severe socio-alcoholic withdrawal, asks me this. "I was just there with some friends from Cocker Spaniel Rescue."

Francie, who, until Bilkie grew pregnant, looked so much like her that she took to prefacing all her conversations by enunciating her name, shushes her loudly. None of these people have ever been suspects before, and likely never will be. They find my life endlessly amusing; I can't imagine a single one of them has committed murder, or ever will.

◆　◆　◆

Daddy finds me. The Stuarts have a buffet and there's live music. A quartet plays sluggish old jazz standards. Together we pass from one cologne to the next as if flipping through the pages of a women's magazine. With the bulk of the furniture out of the way, there's room to dance. We do.

Sometimes I tease Daddy by looking for attention elsewhere, but when we waltz his body fits mine and it feels natural that he's the only man who will ever be my father. We dance, and the biological connection is unmistakable. How do people find attachments among total strangers?

My head is somewhat unaccountable, my thoughts colored pulses that sting when I blink. By no means am I an alcoholic, but I find inebriation helpful in situations such as this. And I only want to drink more with the investigators everywhere and always asking me the same questions, as if I could recall the answers better than they. I suppose I'm naturally somewhat stiff. I think too much. I talk too much, and not of the proper things. Alcohol is an intellectual anesthetic. People tell me I'm a more attractive person when drunk, and it's true. The nasty, jagged edges fall away. Only when intoxicated can I escape impulses I'm not supposed to have. Only when intoxicated am I truly myself.

The quartet is playing "Don't Sit Under the Apple Tree." Daddy guides me across the dance floor. We swirl and dip until breakfast is served.

TWO

I'M CAUGHT WEARING OLD JEANS AND A college sweatshirt when Agents Brody and Emmett appear. I've pinned my unwashed hair in a barrette.

It's Saturday morning. I'm at home only because Emily canceled brunch to accommodate a weekend shoot of Vici Sport's new cross-trainer line. I've been reading old issues of *The Algonquin* since I awoke, although my apartment is a disaster and I've not picked up the living room in weeks. Anybody who keeps clean except for an audience is foolish and vain.

"I wasn't expecting you at all," I tell the agents when I find them at the door to my building. I hate uninvited guests. But to be polite, I ask, "Shall we go for bagels? In the Chestnut?"

Emmett takes the door from my hand while Brody shuffles his feet on the mat and says, "We're coming upstairs."

"Is there a reason? The place is an awful mess, and I haven't a thing in the refrigerator."

"We're not sure we saw everything we needed to the last time."

"It's your own fault for not paying attention. The way you've been ignoring me lately, I was beginning to get used to it."

Brody cocks an eyebrow, hands me some paperwork, and I wonder whether maybe I've said too much. In first grade, my teachers always phoned home to complain about how unruly and disrespectful I'd been during this recess or that nap time, and only because I was a girl and supposed to cry when criticized. But nobody ever taught me to do so convincingly. They still haven't, and that's why for me the only defense is an offense, even if it means offending someone as harmless as Agent Brody.

I try to soften the blow by showing some hospitality, and inevitably I overcompensate. "Would you like something to drink? Would you like . . ." All I see in my refrigerator are bottles of wine. "Can I offer you a glass of Fumé Blanc?"

"At ten A.M.?"

"Is it so criminal?" I pour myself a glass. "Maybe you'd prefer a Pinot Grigio . . ." But already they're in the living room, stepping over the books and papers on the floor.

"It's an ideal arrangement, really." I catch up to them, wine in hand. "Because the French doors open directly into the dining room, so you can have thirty people or more to a party, but overnight guests can still be set up in relative privacy."

I point out the bookshelves, large and glass-covered. Daddy took them with him when he left UC San Francisco for private practice, and then he gave them to me. "I hope you won't have to report him," I whisper.

"That's not the sort of thing that worries us presently, Gloria," Brody says while Emmett takes dictation on his notepad. "Although we always appreciate your candor."

◆   ◆   ◆

Only after I'd put in real time as a suspect did I earn the trust of Brody and Emmett, and did we develop some familiarity. Lately they even ask my advice.

I'm good for them, and I suspect that when I'm not around they don't get along so well. This is their first investigation together. Emmett was just shipped from the D.C. office. He's easily excitable and built like a golden retriever: stocky and covered with hair. His flesh is as soft as a layer of cake against his bones. His clothing never fits. Emmett taught himself to pick locks in junior high school. He got thrown out of college for setting up infrared cameras in women's studies professors' bedrooms and screening the results in his sociology class. Agent Brody has stories, too, but he always leaves off midsentence and lets Emmett talk instead. I know that Brody studied philosophy in school and wanted to become an independent filmmaker. I know that his head is large and round and offset from his body like a golf ball on a tee. I know that Brody is unable to explain, apparently even to himself, how he ended up as a G-man. Of course, I have my suspicions.

I take them through the French doors to my dining room. The table's a country-rustic piece dating from the turn of the century. Both are particularly impressed by the hand-blacksmithed nails. Presumably I was, too, once, although at the moment I can't concentrate on anything but their reactions to my surroundings, and it's almost like watching a new lover stumble through my life. Do they see parts of me that I've forgotten? Know more about me than I know about myself? I study the hand-blacksmithed nails, too. Know your enemy and know yourself. I try to see iron as evidence.

"It's all very nice of you, Gloria, the time you're taking, but I think we'll be okay on our own now." Agent Brody is speaking. He scratches his large blond head while his partner struggles with a crooked necktie.

"Nonsense. I'm having . . . fun."

Brody gives me a weak smile, and I suspect he'd like to be drinking Fumé Blanc too, despite the hour and the circumstances. "Did PJ have a favorite room?" he asks at last, seeing that I'll not go away.

I lead them into the bedroom. "Why would PJ have a favorite room in my apartment?" I sit on the bed, place the glass of wine on the floor between my bare feet. Both Brody and Emmett are staring, admiring the thirty-dollar pedicure. As PJ had. "Do *you* have a favorite room in my apartment?"

"PJ was here often," Emmett clarifies.

"You've been, too. Twice. Not that I don't thrill in your company."

"You and PJ had a . . . relationship." Brody again. Emmett's on hands and knees. He's found the stash of condoms in the drawer of my night table. The condoms are classified by type. I try to keep a stock of both ribbed and smooth and to have each available with and without lubrication, all in their candy-colored packets with their soft-porn names. I glance at Emmett. Smile. I think I see him blush.

"PJ was my employer. Most people have . . . relationships with their employers."

"Sexual ones?"

I glance at Emmett again. He's putting the condoms back into the drawer. He won't look at me.

"Is that a sociological question? I don't think I qualify as an expert witness, but I suppose we can initiate a small-scale study among ourselves. Agent Emmett, how many times a week do you screw your boss?"

"This isn't a sociological question, Gloria. It isn't even a hypothetical one. We already know you and PJ had a relationship outside the office."

"Already know what? Did PJ tell you? Because I certainly didn't, and I hardly think PJ was the sort to fornicate for an audience." I sip my wine. "Now remind me why this is relevant."

"How, Gloria," Emmett asks from his place on the floor, "would you characterize your relationship with your father?"

"Purely sexual."

Emmett slams his hand on the nightstand. Brody ignores him and goes on. "Purely sexual?" he asks.

"Daddy . . . PJ . . . With each, the pleasures were so different and yet so similar." I smile.

Brody chuckles. Stops. "You really should take us more seriously, Gloria. What we're asking is, just how much hands-on knowledge do you have of anatomy?"

"I'm educated."

Brody persists, "How, exactly?" Behind him I see Emmett refolding sweaters in my closet. "Can you identify all the major bones in the leg, say?"

"Don't patronize me."

"How about an oblique fracture to the clavicle? Were you, for example, performing a dissection, could you diagnose an oblique fracture to the clavicle?"

"I thought Rake was still on vacation in Sun Valley."

"He is."

"Enjoying himself, I hope." I'll have to commend him for his honesty when he returns. Nothing is more detrimental to a magazine than a staff that tries to cover for its editor. Competent liars are rare, and a little incompetence goes a long way when there's a criminal investigation involved. "Did you know that I'm also a cannibal?"

"You haven't answered the question, Gloria. The medical records that report a fractured clavicle have been sealed since PJ's autopsy, and you've never had an opportunity to examine the body—at least since it was recovered. Which makes us wonder how you knew his clavicle has an oblique fracture."

"As any first-year med student can tell you, the clavicle is one of the most fragile bones in the body. Due to the muscle structure of the shoulder, the fracture is nearly always oblique. If someone complains of shoulder pain and limited arm movement, it's a pretty easy diagnosis to make. This is basic stuff, Agent Brody. You'd think an FBI agent would know better."

"You're not an FBI agent."

"I considered being a doctor."

"Did PJ complain to you often?" Emmett wriggles out from under my bed. He's holding my copy of *Crime and Punishment.* And another object. He blushes when I brush his back with my foot, but he persists. "Was that one of the ways in which you were . . . close?"

"I was a good employee. I was there for him, in every way." I smile at Emmett. Invitingly. "Is medical diagnosis now classified as sexual activity?" I stand. I take his fist in my hands and open it like an expensive present. PJ's personal phone card, the one he lent to me while I was still an intern, that I used diligently for the next three years, flashing silver like a caught fish, drops to the floor. Brody moves his body between us. He takes the card away.

"You *ass*hole." I look over at my copy of *Crime and Punishment.* "That was my bookmark."

THREE

T WAS IN ONE OF THOSE POSTCOITAL moments when the silence becomes unbearable that PJ told me he's heard back from *The Algonquin*. We were in my apartment, on top of my unmade bed. I was drunk and naked and lying beside the warm, hard wall his body formed between us.

He wouldn't look at me when he spoke. "It didn't happen," he said.

I rolled toward him. I placed my chin on his shoulder. "Don't do this to me, PJ. I'll never forgive you if you're lying."

"And if I'm telling the truth?"

"It's impossible," I answered, but I could feel my skin going tight as I spoke, and I knew he was being honest. "What will you do?"

"What do you think I'll do, Gloria?" He turned his face to me.

"We had an agreement." I pulled the sheets to my body

and still I felt cold. I sat up. I sat against my headboard with my quilt balled against my chest. "We had an *agree*ment, PJ."

"There were conditions."

"I did not stick around *Portfolio* as fucking food editor to have to deal with conditions. Just because you're not good enough for *The Algonquin* doesn't mean—"

"It does, Gloria." PJ reached out one of his hands toward me. I brushed it away. I pulled my legs to my chest and buried my face between my knees.

"Don't fucking touch me!"

"I agreed to back you as editor of *Portfolio* only if I landed *The Algonquin*. Nobody forced you to stick around for two years. If I were you, I'd have grabbed that senior editorship at *Gourmet* when they offered it. You knew you were taking a risk."

"I don't take risks. This isn't how it was presented to me, PJ. You told me you'd be hired. You lied to me." I kicked him in the side with my heel. "You're a lying shit and I won't tolerate it."

"Gloria, this is the top position at *The Algonquin* we're talking about. Every editor in the country was after it the day Will O'Shaugnessy announced his retirement. My chances were about as good as . . . your chances of winning a Pulitzer. You knew there were no guarantees."

"I guess I believed in you, PJ." I sighed, then took a tumbler of bourbon from my nightstand and slowly rotated it in my hands. I splashed the contents across his body. "If you can't get a job at *The Algonquin,* what makes you think you're good enough for *Portfolio?* Or me?"

It wasn't the sort of question he was prepared to answer, so we fucked again, this time with me on top. But of course it wasn't the same. Sex was our conspiracy, our secret handshake, and what passion there was came from the solidarity of two people hopelessly in love with themselves. Once that was gone, sleeping together lost its purpose. His penis felt slick and dumb inside me, and what kept us going to the bitter end can only have been editorial instinct.

"You realize this can't continue," I remarked as I rolled the condom off his prick and tossed it in his face. "I expect payback, and I will collect."

Of course, I didn't go into detail. I explored my options, as any good editor does. I went to the UC San Francisco medical library the next morning. I've always been fascinated with toxicology, and was actively considering a story on the red tide.

I believe strongly in primary sources for two reasons: accuracy and originality. Some criminals rely on movies for their background information when planning a murder. These are the people who only do damage to those they aspire to kill, and inevitably get caught in the process. Why should a screenwriter bother to calculate *how much* chloroform is needed to knock out a character? Does it weaken the plot if the chemistry's off? People don't care if the specifics are right, just so long as there are specifics. Realism and accuracy seldom have any correlation.

And then there's originality. The public may not know much about toxicology, but it does know its Alfred Hitchcock. Who wants to poison someone as seen on TV? Plagiarism is dirty and demeaning. Murder, like magazine editing, is a creative act. It must be executed with authority.

Of course, medical books are unwieldy, and lay research is only productive if you understand the texts' intended purpose. Think Hippocratic Oath: *First do no harm.* Those books are about how to diagnose and to treat overdoses, not how to administer them. They're cautious in their estimations. If they claim that .1 mg/kg of a given barbiturate is fatal, you're better off administering five to ten times that amount. There is no certainty in medicine. The trick is to find those drugs with the strongest clinical correlation between administration and fatality.

Take the case of neuromuscular blocking agents. These are used primarily during surgical anesthesia to promote muscle relaxation, as well as to control convulsions. The beauty is that, in large enough doses, blocking agents cause both respiratory paralysis and circulatory collapse. If you set the quantity right, the whole messy process of death can be reduced to mere minutes. Vecuronium bromide is the most potent blocking agent on the market, requiring a dose of only .08 mg/kg to induce total respiratory paralysis. If your subject can't breathe, he dies. Suffocation does that to you.

Medical references are somewhat more prissy when it comes to matters postmortem. Forensics, however, isn't so shy. All the information you need to commit an undetectable crime, if not the perfect one, is fully indexed in those workaday texts.

Postmortem injury, for example, is of interest to investigators in cases where murderers try to cover up their work by fabricating a struggle after the fact. Or, in other words, when they try to turn first-degree murder into second-degree or even manslaughter. The tip-off? Once the heart stops, serious bleeding does as well.

I once saw a photograph of a man who died in his apartment and wasn't found for days. He had a small dog. The dog ate most of the flesh from his face. When he was discovered, he had a beard of exposed muscle. There was no blood, no clotting or spillage. Just his face, liplessly grinning, as clean as licked fingers.

Forensics books are eager to please: blood and hair and clothing fibers and lipstick all make good evidence, but only when there's a suspect to match them up against. The FBI keeps records of these things, as well as of tire tracks, shoe prints, cigarettes, automobile paint, and safe insulation. Debris found on site can be matched up against it to determine brand information, which is again only useful when there's a defined group of suspects. Even fingerprints have their limitations: they do little good if the perpetrator is an employee, relative, or friend, since the fingerprints of any of the above will likely be on the scene of the crime before the crime was ever committed.

The equipment the FBI has is sophisticated and sensitive, but totally useless if one follows a few simple rules. You'd think it might make the perfect topic for an article, maybe even a cover story. A few days later I proposed the idea to PJ. He told me it wasn't credible.

FOUR

PERRY NASH SAYS IT DOESN'T MATTER that he's late, because love conquers all. Men assume the queerest things once you've fucked them, even if only on a single occasion and while drunk. Sometimes they can't understand how sex can be just another transaction. Men can be so sentimental.

I show Perry my watch. I unbuckle it from my wrist. I hand it to him across my desk and explain, "You were supposed to be here when the little hand was on the three and the big hand was on the twelve. Can you tell me where the little hand is now?"

"I thought I was a priority."

"I have other appointments, Perry. They're priorities, too."

"Let me guess: critical meeting with your manicurist."

"Florist."

"My mistake." He reaches into his alligator-skin doctor's bag. "Fortunately, I know you better than you think." He extracts an elaborate bouquet. Bunched tight in his enormous hands. Muscular hands, like Daddy's. "That's why I'm late,

Gloria. The first letter of each flower represents a letter in your name. I was late because I got stuck on *o*."

"Orchid? Oregon grape holly?"

"You're good." He grins, and his whole face crinkles like aluminum foil.

I pluck the bouquet from his fists and drop it into my umbrella stand. I hold out my hand and request that he return my watch.

"Too late. I've taken it as a token of your affection." He holds it to his heart, then drops it into his pocket. "Anyway, it'll cost you. Transactions, Gloria. I'm sure you can relate."

"You realize that watch belonged to PJ. He gave it to me."

"You have to appreciate the perversity."

"I doubt he would." In the end, PJ refused to talk to Perry, and told Spivvy to call security if he ever showed up at the office. Of course it was an article that caused the rift, and of course I should have known better than to bring Perry back. But Perry Nash is connected, and certain articles require the sort of credentials that only his sort can offer. An M.D. who still remembers the rules of grammar, let alone one familiar with the niceties of investigative journalism, is rare.

Perry knows how precious a find he is, and that's the difficulty. He complains bitterly about rewrites and threatens lawsuits over changed syntax. Which explains why PJ ultimately killed his exposé on breast cancer misdiagnosis.

I heard their fights. Everybody did.

Perry asks why I'm letting him write for me now. Why, if I think PJ was right about him, I'd take him to bed with me.

"Mood-altering drugs are different, Perry. Nobody's done a story on their recreational possibilities. In any case, I had to fuck you. That was your price for working with me."

"Wasn't it good for you?"

"Based on the evidence here, no." I slide his article across my desk, bloody with my ink.

Perry ignores it. Counters, "I think what you need is some Prozac." He reaches into his breast pocket for his prescription pad. "Pick a dosage."

"It wouldn't help." Doctors always try to prescribe me Prozac or give me other drugs. As if mere chemicals could make me happier. Why should I want to be content?

"I don't understand, Gloria."

"I don't, either, and that's the problem. Your story has nothing to do with recreational mood-altering."

"What do you mean?"

"You devote over a thousand words to your upbringing in San Diego."

"Um."

"You bring up the specter of serotonin without explaining its function. You promise to explain the National Ritalin Exchange and then never—"

"But I love you, Gloria. You're such a terrific screw."

"I am your editor." I fold the article and hand it to him. "Rewrite it. I'll need another draft by Tuesday." I smile. "By the way, the FBI has some interesting theories. They said your article was pure self-promotion. Autobiography." I drop my chin into my palm. "Nevertheless, you may be useful."

He asks whether I gave them his name.

"They're friends. They don't care. Brody and Emmett are just looking out for me."

"Are you still a suspect?" he asks.

"You know the case as well as I do."

"What's that supposed to mean?"

"You read the papers."

"No time for that." He stands. "I just cut out the pictures of you."

FIVE

WHAT MAKES EMILY A SUPERIOR HOSTESS is that she curates her parties. Every invitation is carefully considered before it's sent. I help her with the screening process. The procedure is not unlike choosing stories for a magazine.

It's New Year's Eve. Twenty-five couples have been selected. People mingle.

I see Emily roll her eyes when she takes my coat, although I've already told her Dmitri was to be my date. I've brought him because I'm not currently seeing anyone with whom I'm prepared to be seen, and this year PJ was unavailable. Being a suspected murderer is like being royalty or an athlete or a movie star. I am a public figure; Dmitri is my bodyguard.

Deirdre, of course, is the first to spot us. She's already impressively drunk. She's with Jerry, who's impressively sober. She's been dating Jerry for under a week. She calls him her fiancé and has already made him buy her a gold bracelet and two pair of shoes. The trouble is that he won't leave her alone at parties. Only in bed.

Emily reappears. She hands me a scotch and Dmitri a martini. He bows when he thanks her.

Max comes by, with his wife, Nina. Max works with Emily, and I know him because he's always at her parties. Sometimes he brings Nina. Sometimes he brings his boyfriend, whose name is also Max. Sometimes they all come together and laugh a lot and don't leave until after everyone else has gone home.

Nina and Deirdre appraise people's dresses. Max and Dmitri discuss how brilliant an editor I am. Emily drags me into the kitchen with her.

"What are you doing?" I hiss when the door swings shut. "They were talking about me."

"You're so conceited."

"And?"

"You promised me you wouldn't bring him."

"Bring who?"

"The fucking Russian, Glor."

"Does it matter? Deirdre brought Jerry."

"Jerry isn't fat and ugly. Jerry isn't fifty plus." Emily washes used glassware. She tosses me a towel. "Jerry doesn't make my party look like a fucking Ellis Island reunion."

"Who was I supposed to bring? Daddy?"

"I work so hard at these parties, Glor. You *always* do this to me." She hands me a tumbler to dry. The water warms my towel. "Why can't you pick on dates your own age? Why can't you be . . . ordinary?"

"You know the answer to that, Emily."

"How about *Perry*?"

"Still a fucking disaster. Pretty soon I won't even be able to get laid."

"Tell me." She turns off the sink. Leans against the counter with her arms crossed.

"I guess I'm not superficial enough to believe his lovey-dovey bullshit. It's contagious. Spreading over the whole male species. I can only imagine the result will be extinction."

"You're so dramatic, Glor."

"Of course Perry's trying to get me in bed with him again." I'm drying glasses still. The same glasses I dried before. Emily takes away the cloth. "But you know how it ends. I mean, there are ways to fake it. Deirdre does. She's engaged for the third time this year and she doesn't know Jerry any better than I do. I think it has to do with suspension of disbelief. With lying to yourself and saying there's more than can ever be. I'm too honest for that. I simply can't pretend."

"But with the Russian—"

"Don't you see that Dmitri's different, Em? It's like passing counterfeit money at the bank." I know because I've spent real money before, spent it freely, even generously.

"That doesn't sound very honest, Glor."

"Dmitri doesn't want the real thing. Real money has consequences. Didn't your father ever show you . . . Do you understand what I'm saying?"

"Of course I do, Gloria." She stacks a tray with tumblers and another with highballs. She kisses my cheek. "Help me carry?"

I grasp the edge of a tray. "You're not listening to me."

"I *am* listening to you." She pushes her way past the kitchen door. I follow. "But the counterfeit Russian is loose in my living room. And I won't have him traumatizing my guests."

She's right to worry. While we unload glasses onto the sideboard, I overhear Dmitri lecturing Max, and Nina, too. "It proves nothing, the telephone card. PJ and Gloria were close. He left the card behind once when they were visiting. When he discovered its loss, he called the phone company to make a cancellation."

"He didn't notice for over a year?"

"There was no rupture in their relationship before PJ's life ended. You should not believe what you read. I saw them together to the end. He was her mentor. When he was gone, I hired her to replace him."

Dmitri thinks it was the FBI who leaked the phone-card story to the press. He doesn't understand public relations. Self-incrimination only makes people want to believe you're innocent.

But he's doing his job. Making himself useful to me.

I leave him. Emily's playing tango now, turning up the volume every time she passes her stereo. Somebody unfamiliar requests a dance with me. I say yes, but there's no room. I keep swallowing tumblers of scotch, each one fuller, hazier. Deirdre keeps running back and forth to the bathroom, shooting tequila and throwing up. Jerry's upset because Deirdre won't let him in the bathroom with her. "She could drown," he insists.

"She usually doesn't."

"Isn't it nearly midnight?"

"Why?"

"I want to be with my fiancée."

"Then practice being a toilet." I smile, but the countdown begins in earnest and he's gone already.

And then it's midnight. Several men kiss me because they don't know me and I don't know them. I kiss them back, longer and harder than they expect. One of them puts his hand on my ass. I take what remains of his champagne and return his glass to him when I'm through. Transactions. Good sex feels like success or like committing the perfect crime, but it doesn't matter because there's nothing left in the morning. Mostly I don't feel it anyway.

The room wobbles when I move. I find I have a cigarette in my hand. Somebody lights it.

It's Dmitri.

"Why are you ignoring me?" he asks, his accent fortified by his vodka.

He looks upset. I kiss him anyway, parting his lips with my tongue. "You've been smoking *cigars.*"

"That's not the point. Why are you ignoring me, Gloria? Leaving me standing alone like you don't want to be seen with me?"

"I haven't a clue what you're talking about. I hate cigarettes. Do you have more cigars? For me?" I drain the rest of my drink, inhale on my Dunhill until my lungs hurt, and blow all the smoke in his face. Dmitri is large and round and built like a reptile. His face is bigger than a dinner plate. "Some men find that sexy," I comment.

"You're drunk," Dmitri says, as if it's some sort of revelation, something neither of us grasped before that promises to make everything much clearer. "That's what I don't understand about you, Gloria. You drink and then you act like a child."

I exhale in his face again. Giggling.

"You stop that, Gloria." He stomps his foot. His puffy hands open and close like sea anemones. He looks ready to cry.

"You stop that and listen to me. I'm much older than you. There are things I know that you don't."

"Like what?" By squinting, I find I can make Dmitri multiply.

"Your generation, I don't understand. You never pay attention."

"I listen, just not to insensitive *ass*holes who don't refill my drinks or offer me cigars when I need them." If I move my head quickly, I can make Dmitri swerve and dip, following the ever-changing contours of the room. "Weren't you just telling Max how talented I am?"

"You are talented. That's what makes me sad. You don't learn from others. From me."

"If you don't get me another drink, I'm sure I can find someone else who will."

Dmitri takes my glass. I follow him to the bar, which under other circumstances is Emily's dining room table. She's draped white sheets over everything for the party. Emily has always imagined herself an interior decorator.

Dmitri only fills the glass partway. I take the bottle from him and top it off. "What'll you have? The same?" Dmitri says nothing. I fill another glass with scotch and hand it to him. Out of habit, he nods.

"Now what were you saying?"

"I was telling you that you should be more like PJ."

"Dead, you mean?"

"That's not appropriate, Gloria. You need to have more tact."

"Fuck you. I *do* have tact."

"Not enough."

"More than anybody else."

"Why do you have to compare yourself to everybody else?"

"*You* compare me to everybody else." As I say this, I top off my scotch again, stopping only when I can feel the alcohol trickling over my hand. I put the drink down. I wipe my fingers on Dmitri's blood-red cummerbund.

"I have a lot of respect for you, Gloria."

"You're an asshole." I lift the drink to my face but at first can't locate my mouth. With a handkerchief colored to match his tux, Dmitri wipes the flow of scotch from my chin before it streaks my clothing.

"I just want the magazine not to suffer now that PJ's gone."

"PJ wasn't the best editor," I point out.

"Maybe not. But he was loyal."

"Bullshit!" I can feel my face going hot and cold at once. "Loyalty didn't stop him from interviewing with *The Algonquin.*"

"But he stayed with me."

"That's because he didn't have a choice, Dmitri. He'd have been out of his fucking mind to turn them down."

"PJ was a hard worker. He was always at the office late. He would lecture at journalism schools."

"Will you please stop changing the subject. Why are you doing this to me? You're supposed to be my *date.*"

I reach for the bottle of scotch again. Dmitri covers the top of my glass with his palm. I clamp my free hand around his fat wrist and tell him that if he doesn't stop I'm going to fucking scream.

Perhaps sensing the mounting tension on our side of the room, Emily comes by with a tray of champagne flutes. She smiles.

"Have some more Dom, Glor. Somebody opened all the bottles. Wouldn't want it to spoil." I balance my tumbler on her tray. I take two glasses and glower when Dmitri tries to remove one from my hands.

"I'm going to the roof," I announce, without directing the comment to anybody. Dmitri is acrophobic.

At the top of the stairs, a cooler has been put out, and in it are more opened bottles of Dom. A man named Rocky is filling people's glasses. Some are Steuben, like Emily's, but there are others: Baccarat, Lalique, Mikasa. The cooler could be anybody's. There must be five or six parties in Emily's building, all overflowing onto the roof. Dmitri is gone. I find myself in a quick lot of conversations with neighboring guests. Mostly I tell them what a fucking nightmare it is having to entertain the FBI while they crawl around my apartment, trying to find wayward calling cards.

Eventually, I notice Deirdre standing by my side. She seems oddly out of context.

"Will you hold my feet while I puke off the roof?"

"Puke?"

"Off the roof. I'd go back to the apartment, but if I throw up on the way, I'll slip. I'll fall down the staircase."

The roof has no railing. She lies down, head over the edge. Gravel digs into my knees as I grasp her ankles. Nobody sees and nobody hears.

I could let her drop without a witness.

SIX

MY STEPFATHER, SIDNEY, IS IN HIS living room, speaking with his stockbroker in the stripped English of the Brooklyn ghetto circa 1950, so fashionable now among upper-middle-class bearded Jews living in California. Mostly it's a matter of vocabulary: certain words are said in Yiddish, and if you get the accent right it blends with the English into an unending drone not unlike the sound of prayer. *Mensch* and *meshuggener*. *Yid* and *goy*. How easily the world divides.

Today there's little need for the distinction, though, because Sidney only invites *mensches* to New Year's brunch. He sometimes lets my mother add a few names to the list. I was her top choice.

"Now, my daughter Gloria," Sidney's saying, as always ignoring the essential distinction that we're not related by blood, "she's a nice Jewish girl. She doesn't look Jewish, but that's okay. What I don't understand is what she's doing in the middle of this murder. I keep telling her that Jewish girls don't work in places where people get killed, she should get out while she still can, and they certainly don't let themselves become suspects. But she won't listen."

"I'm not *that* kind of suspect. I talk to the FBI a couple of times a week. I try to help them with their case."

"Why don't you just get married? How many times have I suggested that you go to Young Singles' Night at the JCC? You spend all your time with goyim."

"Maybe, Sidney, it's because I'm an anti-Semite."

I escape to the backyard, which is where the smokers congregate at Sidney's parties. The smokers aren't a bad bunch when compared with the nonsmokers. There's Herman Weiss, the meat wholesaler, and David Hertzberg, the insurance adjuster. There are Larry Stein and Barry Reischbach, both lawyers. And there's Barry's wife, Judy, who owns a shop specializing in antique Judaica and handcrafted Israeli tchotchkes.

Barry, who used to be in criminal law, is telling me stories about the clients whose executions he attended. He says the gas chamber is quick, but the electric chair offers a better show.

We talk about Agent Brody's disproportionately large head. Barry and Brody have crossed paths before, although they've not seen each other since Barry's son's bar mitzvah.

"Just remember. You have an attorney if you need me for anything."

"I can't imagine why." I sip my seltzer and attempt to look as though I mean it. Suspension of disbelief. It's something I really must learn. "I'm not much good as a criminal. Guilt and innocence seem so . . . remote."

"The guys in D.C. love to harass people, Gloria. Why do you think they want to subpoena phone company records on

PJ's calling card? Your friends' phone numbers have nothing to do with their case—but plenty to do with your personal life. They try to spook you into confessing, the FBI. That's why I switched to copyright law. Criminal cases aren't fun for *any*-body."

I nod and smile and look beautiful and then my mother makes me come inside with her so she can show me off. "You're so shy, Gloria. If it weren't for me, you'd never talk to any-body."

"I talk to people. I talk to them all the time."

She guides me through a tropical forest of guests, orange-, blue-, and green-dressed, muttering their names to me so that when we head in the opposite direction I can pretend I re-member them from the last brunch and I'm so sorry I keep missing them at the kugel klatsch: a whole Torah portion's Abrahams, Isaacs, and Jacobs, Rebeccas, Leahs, and Rachels.

"You ought to take Barry seriously," my mother says. We've stopped at the buffet so she can make me a plate of bagels and lox and kippers and pickled herring.

"I'm not hungry, Mom."

She shrugs. Frail, limp features, excessively long brown hair: surely there aren't many genes we hold in common. "Barry knows a lot about criminal law, Gloria. He's defended some important murderers." She adds a second layer of cream cheese to the bagels. "He's highly regarded by Sidney."

"I'm really not hungry."

"You know his son is a lawyer, too. Already a partner at Hoojiwhatsits & Hoojiwoo . . . You know, that big firm down-town."

"I don't want to date his son." I bite into one of the bagels. I bite some more, and pretty soon it's gone.

"Sidney says Barry's son may be nominated BART commissioner. He thinks you two would have so much to talk about."

"And Sidney knows me so well." I eat the kippers. I despise overcooked fish. When I talk, my mouth is full of kippers and pickled herring, which makes my lips pucker. "If you weren't married to Sidney, Mom, I'd marry him myself."

"I understand he's not your father . . ."

"Please don't start." I prepare another bagel, this time with lox and onion and capers.

"You're so quick to take offense, dear. I only want what's best for you."

"Which is where Sidney comes in." I drag all the lox into my mouth when I bite into the bagel. Capers bounce on the floor.

"He's not so bad. Once you get used to him."

"You've been saying that for fifteen years."

"During which you've been here how many times?"

"Weren't you going to introduce me to your friends?" I remind her, sliding the plate under the table to prevent myself from eating more.

"You already know these people, Gloria." She grasps my arm. "Please try to remember their names."

But already I've forgotten. I'm a suspected murderer. I have the right to remain silent.

SEVEN

DEIRDRE ANNOUNCES SHE HAS POSI-
tively no clothes. We've just stepped into Macy's
Union Square. "Come with me so I can try things
on," she pesters.

I tell her she'll have to wait her turn. I tell her I want to
make my returns first, and that's why we're here. She hasn't
finished making her Christmas exchanges, either, but she's not
as meticulous about these things as I am. Sometimes she leaves
bags of undesirable gifts in bathrooms or dressing rooms or the
offices of people she's never met. This is Deirdre's way of being
charitable. The holiday spirit and all that.

Deirdre follows me to basement-level cookware, naming the
garments she intends to acquire before we're through: boiled-
wool skirts and white cotton T-shirts and striped V-neck tennis
sweaters. I ignore her. I show the chrome teapot I've come to return to a clerk in an enormous bow tie. He says he needs to check
the price. Explains that he just transferred from china.

"I didn't know there were department stores in the Orient," Deirdre loudly interrupts. "*Gung hay fat choy. I love* potstickers."

"He meant he'd transferred from the china *department,* Deir," I whisper when he disappears to check on kitchenware prices. "Not the People's Republic."

"Oh." She looks at the teapot. "Where did you get that?"

"It's why we're standing here now. It's the teapot I was trying to return when you assaulted the poor clerk with your Q-and-A about potstickers."

"I did not Q-and-A him about potstickers. I told him how much I *like* potstickers. There's a difference."

"So. There's a difference."

She reaches across the counter, on tiptoes. She takes the teapot in her hands, cradling it like a pet. "Where did it come from?"

"One of the FBI agents, if you can believe it. He's in love with me."

"In love with you?"

"What I can't believe is that the other one didn't buy me something, too. I'm always so nice to him."

"He's an *FBI* agent, Glor. He's investigating a murder case, and you're the main suspect. He's not supposed to buy you things. I don't think the other one is, either. You haven't been making promises again? You're not sleeping with him?"

"No. I'm accommodating. That's all. I bought them both Filofaxes for Christmas. I taught them all about calendars, so maybe they'll make an appointment the next time they want to search my apartment." I try to take the teapot back from Deirdre. She won't let go.

"*I* need a chrome teapot," she says.

"Then buy one."

"But you're returning this—"

"What's it going to look like if Agent Emmett finds out I gave you his teapot? If he finds it in your apartment."

"Why would he be in my apartment?"

"He was in mine."

"So?"

"You're a friend. Maybe even an accomplice. They're so desperate for clues lately, those two. There's no knowing what significance they could read into a teapot." But I let go. It's hers now. Just like everything she wants.

"What happened when he gave it to you?"

"I said thank you."

"That's all?" She examines her trophy more carefully.

"It's not like I fucked him for a kettle. This is totally platonic. I'm not Sharon Stone, you know."

"He's in love with you."

"More or less. I think he'd have given me back PJ's phone card when he found it, too. If Agent Brody hadn't seen."

"Agent Brody doesn't like you."

"He's shy. He likes me in his own way."

The clerk is back. On a fragment of paper, he's jotted down some numbers. "Will you wrap this for me, Mr. Chinaman?" Deirdre smiles at him. Hands him the teapot.

"Ex*cuse*?"

"Just a standard Macy's box will do. Red bow. And one of those nice bags with handles." She turns back to me. "You're so narcissistic. Are you sure this is the best defense, having your investigators lusting after you?" She takes the bag from the clerk. Bows. Together we take the escalator back upstairs. "Love is a fickle thing."

"You're forgetting that I'm beautiful."

Her face creases. "I worry. That something will happen and it will just be Emily and me."

Deirdre leaves me in women's wear. She leaves me to try on silk blouses. I exchange a bouillabaisse of fishnet stockings Perry Nash sent me for Christmas. I trade them in for a scarf I think Daddy will like. Lately he complains I'm not dressing nicely. He won't take me to any good restaurants. He doesn't hug me except after he's had two or three drinks.

From behind the dressing room door, I hear Deirdre complaining about Jerry. In all likelihood, it's me she's addressing, but her voice is loud enough for people in men's furnishings to hear. "I had to spend the night at Emily's. The little fuck went home with Max while I was passed out in the coat closet. I broke off our engagement, but I get to keep the bracelet anyway. Did you screw the Russian?"

"I think I woke up alone."

"You shouldn't have made me hurl off her roof, Glor. It was all over Em's walkway the next morning. She was so pissed I had to tell her it was yours."

While she speaks, she gathers more clothing. Over and over, I watch her enter the dressing room with three items and exit with only two, each time looking a little bulkier and moving a bit more awkwardly. She always takes souvenirs when I shop with her, and to make up for the inconvenience she gives me some as gifts. This is how I get most of my lingerie.

She systematically works her way through her wardrobe, concentrating on the spring and summer collections. She fits herself with three layers of stirrup pants and then slacks and jeans and skirts and dresses. She finds some boiled wool. I hand her a cardigan I like.

Deirdre say she'll wait outside while I have my new scarf packaged, and I watch her maneuver her bulky body into the elevator. Her little problem growing large. She drops a pair of shoes. She doesn't bother to pick them up.

◆　　◆　　◆

A security guard is interrogating Deirdre in front of hordes of passing shoppers. They're out on the street. She's crying, although not so convincingly as usual.

"What happened?" I ask, passing through the revolving door.

"They accused me of . . . shoplifting. They called the fucking Stasi." She pulls her hands away when he tries to cuff her. "Don't touch me. Do I look like a fucking criminal?"

"She does have a point," I comment to the officer.

"She's wearing six layers of brand-new clothing under that outfit."

"How do you know?"

"They said so inside. And she can hardly walk."

"He has a point, too." I turn to Deirdre. She glares at me. "Maybe you should return that clothing."

"It's January. It's cold out here." She wraps her arms around her body and shivers.

I turn back to the security guard. I shrug. "Well, I guess that's your answer, Officer. I think the technical term is *layering*." I smile at him and look beautiful. "Come along, Deirdre. We haven't got all day."

I push Deirdre into an oncoming school of tourists and we pretend to shoot fake cameras.

When we're across Union Square and the security guard's

gone and the store's gone, too, Deirdre gives me a kiss. She kisses me on the lips and we giggle.

"I always forget how good you are in these situations."

"But I was perfectly honest," I respond. The best explanations merely repackage the truth.

She rolls her eyes.

"I never lie. I think it's why they love me so much."

"Who?"

"The FBI. Telling the truth is very seductive."

"And you're willing to stake your life on it."

"Does it matter?"

"I don't think they're in love with you, Glor. Not both of them and maybe neither one. A chrome teapot isn't exactly an engagement ring."

"You think I can't keep the interest of two fucking FBI agents?" Deirdre always was envious of me. "What should I do instead? What would you propose?"

"Legal help?"

"Then you believe I'm guilty?" I take the teapot back from her. A pair of shoes tumbles from beneath her overcoat. "My life isn't as simple as yours."

"Because you need to be in more newspapers than Abigail Van Buren?"

"My career requires a high profile. Magazine circulation depends on it. That's why I'm lecturing in L.A. next week. And why I consent to grueling interviews the likes of which you've never had to worry about."

"I'm happy with my life. Not everybody needs a murder investigation."

"Not everybody wants to be a human resources tool at a fucking bank when they're sixty-five." But it's too much.

Deirdre doesn't have my advantages, and so she's not as prepared for honesty as I am. I fill the void by reminding her of
my generosity. "I'm glad you took the teapot, Deir. Agent
Emmett isn't my type."

EIGHT

DO YOU ALWAYS TAKE SCOTCH AT FIVE in the afternoon?" Brian Edward Reed-Arnold asks me from across the table. We are at Sea of Hats, a hopelessly bland financial district way station for high-income dipsomaniacs.

"Only when I want to be drunk."

"And you want to be drunk tonight?"

"It wouldn't hurt."

The waiter brings our liquor. Predictably, Brian has ordered a G&T. He pays with well-worn hands. We stare at each other. Of course this was his idea, drinks after work. Noblesse oblige is so much more palatable when you're beautiful like me. Or connected like him.

"So, tell me about sailing," I attempt.

"About sailing?"

"You know, America's Cup and all that."

"I don't really know anything about sailing. I . . . don't

sail." He gives me that helpless look men do when they're caught with nothing to say. "Why do you ask? Do you sail?"

This is not as I intended. Brian is supposed to know about sailing because if he doesn't, I haven't a clue what he knows about. That's the whole reason men wear ties that evoke their favorite sport, or wristwatches that depict their hobbies, or rings that list their college, with major and year of graduation. Men like to be asked about what interests them. Their clothing provides women with speaking points, and when it doesn't, there's nothing to say. Does Brian play golf? Tennis? Polo? Does he ride horses with Art Reingold? I excuse myself and hurry to the ladies' room.

I emerge to find the place pleasantly crowded. The bar, one of those heavy oak beasts that Americans think look so British and Britons know are American, is packed. With everybody dressed in the same color palette, though, it's impossible to say where one ends and where the next begins. Like pigeons, they all look alike.

The same can be said of those sitting at the tables around ours. I note with some irritation that a number of the women have their hair cut as I do. They wear my clothing and my jewelry, too. Perhaps one of them *is* me and I'm one of them. I put a hand to my face. I'm relieved to feel the pressure of my touch.

A new drink is waiting at my place. As far as I can tell, Brian remains diligently on his first. There's a basket of breadsticks on the table. He's eating one. There's a pot of butter, too.

"You really don't know *any*thing about *The Algonquin* editorship? Art Reingold never said a word about what he's looking for?" I ask, giving up on the charade. "I hear the magazine is on the verge of collapse."

"I told you it's not the sort of thing he and I discuss."

"What else is there that matters?" I look down at my fingers. "You know PJ was one of the first to apply."

"Then he was killed."

"Don't be so morose. It happens."

We stare at each other. I smile.

"Do you watch wrestling?" he asks at last.

"No."

"I was on the team in college. I won the state championship. But I couldn't exactly go pro after that." He smiles weakly.

"I'm sure you could make it. With practice."

"You're joking."

"I am not." I drink more, hoping that somehow the alcohol will provide my escape from this conversation and ease my return to what matters. "I'm always serious."

But still it isn't enough for him. He has more to say about wrestling, and I've no choice but to listen. I drink and eat breadsticks with butter and I nod at regular intervals.

"You have to make your opponent believe he'll lose. Wrestling is about psychology. It's like chess. That's why the Greeks loved it."

He starts talking about Greece and the places he's been, but that never impresses me. When I was growing up, my father took me everywhere. He made sure I was well enough traveled never to be intimidated in conversation.

"Then you've been to Assisi, too?" Brian tries to appear pleased. "I must tell you about Irkutsk. About my trip to Lake Baikal."

"Did you take the Trans-Siberian Express? Daddy and I did. Didn't the trains smell dreadful? We were in St. Petersburg, too, of course. We were always trying to ditch the tour group and sneak back into the Hermitage while they were busy haggling with the natives over those hideous Soviet Army watches."

I'm not sure how many breadsticks I eat or how many scotches I drink or how many more countries Brian mentions as I eat and drink and lose count of it all. I do know that the waiter is often at our table and that in the end Brian's wallet is slimmer than it was when we started. It's dark out. The bar has become quiet again.

"So, they aren't sending you to jail, are they?" Without the hum of other conversations to fill them out, Brian's stories have lost purpose, pages torn from a discarded magazine. He needs me now. He needs me even if it means taking the focus from him.

"First you have to tell me more about Art Reingold. *Portfolio* does get tiresome. You know, it's inevitable that he hire me. That editorship is my dream job."

"I don't know anything more," he insists, but his voice is too eager.

"Tell me."

"Art doesn't like to be pursued. Considers it presumptuous and impolite. He brought his business to me. Nobody can reach him, not even his secretary. The rumors are true. You'll be standing in line at a bank and he'll just show up. Never once did I have an appointment with him. Or even a phone number." He crumbles a breadstick between his fingers. "There. Now it's your turn."

"I have this theory about the murder." My hair's fallen in front of my eyes. I brush it back with my hands. I stare at the ceiling, tin painted smooth. What color was it first? I let my hair go. I look at him. "As purposeless characters go, atoned

sinners are second only to confirmed saints. To remain interesting, the Bulk Mail Butcher cannot confess. People don't understand, but it would ruin everything."

"But all criminals need to confess eventually." The waiter
returns once more. Brian asks for a receipt. This is business.
The ending is so obvious. "That's the whole point of a mys-
tery."

"You'll never understand me. Does that bother you?"

"Would you like to get some dinner? I've found the perfect
place."

The thought of his voice or mine drawn out over the next
three hours is unbearable. It's all pointless anyway, that much
is clear, but by now it doesn't matter. Another connection to
the greater world. Nothing more. What I really want is a warm
body against mine, an unfamiliar one preferably, in bed with
clean starchy sheets. A body that doesn't remind me of anything in particular, the investigation, Daddy. A body as quick
and mean as junk food. Commitment always diminishes the
pleasure because then I have to be me and sometimes it's just
too daunting.

"Why don't we just go home and fuck?"

◆ ◆ ◆

I have never understood why, historically speaking, women
have so often found themselves politically subservient to men.
Men are simple to understand, and that's an inherent weakness.
Female sexual desire is an ambiguous thing, internal, intro-
verted. Men don't have this advantage. A penis is an obvious
target. In the past, men have refused to sleep with me, but
none have managed to do so once I've had them undressed.

Men aren't at all difficult to control. Which is why I've never understood history.

When Brian and I are safely inside my apartment, I offer him a drink. He declines. I pour myself one anyway. A margarita, but without the ice or the triple sec or the mix. I make him one, too, just in case.

"You drink a lot," Brian observes when I return to the living room.

"That's what my mother says."

"How about your father? He's a doctor."

"It's something we don't talk about." But still there's a pang. I don't like to think about him when I'm with other men.

Brian has taken off his coat and is sitting on the sofa thumbing through old issues of *Portfolio.* I drop my coat on a chair and place the drinks on the coffee table in front of us. The table is an antique *chadansu.* It still has ring stains from my party.

"So, have you tested?" he asked. "For diseases?" I climb on top of him, drink in hand. I sit on his knees.

"Have a sip." I hold the drink to his mouth.

"No, thank you. I've had plenty."

"I never test, Brian. I don't get diseases." I guide one of his hands around my hip. The magazine falls to the floor.

I kiss him.

"You taste like your drink."

"And you smell like your lunch."

"It's like that with me. My skin easily picks up foreign scents."

"Don't you ever shut up?" I slide to the floor between his legs and unzip his pants. What I find is mostly limp, mealy, and white as a root. "You don't know what to do with me, do you?"

"Um."

"Oh, please don't start talking again. It will ruin *every*-thing." I take another swig of tequila. Pull his pants and underwear to his knees. I stroke the insides of his thighs with the palms of my hands. His penis begins to fill.

I take another swig of tequila. The glass is almost empty, too light in my hand. My mouth wet with alcohol, I press my lips to his and find his tongue with my own.

And then I drag Brian to the floor, all dead weight like a cadaver. I lay him on his back. I pull clothing from his body and mine. From Brian's wrist I remove a gold name bracelet. Over his cock I roll a lubricated condom.

I kneel over him, one leg against each of his hips. His penis is fat and stubby and slips out of me when I sit up straight. I keep low, close to him, my mons veneris against his pelvis. I feel his hands encompass my breasts. I come before he does, the feeling as always familiar but new, trickling through me like a change in mood.

When he's finished, I remove his condom. He's red with sweat. My body is heavy and angular and desireless. Like I've gorged myself on Twinkies. I lie against Brian's stomach. "When do we meet with Art?" I ask him.

III. DISSECTION OF THE HIP

Make an incision through the integument along the crest of the ilium to the middle of the sacrum, and thence downward to the tip of the coccyx, and carry a second incision from that point obliquely downward and outward to the outer side of the thigh, four inches below the great trochanter.

—GRAY'S ANATOMY

ONE

THE HALL IS MOBBED WITH STUDENTS.
There aren't enough seats. At the podium stands a
guy with frizzy hair and the braying voice of a con-
sumer advocate. He said at dinner that he was from Philadel-
phia. *Philly.* His name is Howard and he's wearing a bold rep
tie and a double-breasted blazer.

How he ended up as president of the UCLA Journalism Society I will never understand. He tried to explain over dessert.
I escaped to the pay phones. I dialed Daddy, but some woman
picked up.

I can't focus on anything Howard is saying about me, and
when he asks me to the podium I have trouble standing. I'm
very good at talking to microphones and TV cameras, but even
after all the press conferences, live audiences frighten me. I
worry about saying the wrong thing. I worry about causing offense. Criminal investigations have a way of making even in-

nocent bystanders paranoid. Howard reaches out a moist hand to help. Guides me to the lectern.

"I've been invited by the UCLA Journalism Society," I hear my voice creak, "to speak about journalistic integrity at the millennium's end." I gaze at the speech in front of me. Words shuffle around on the page, sliding in and out of focus as if on an eye chart. "A quaint concept, journalistic integrity. Rather like criminal justice."

My eyes sweep the room. Most in the audience are wearing shorts and T-shirts. Their shirts advertise various fraternities, political causes, local businesses. I glance down at myself and wonder what I look like to them. I'm only four or five years older than most. But they're different somehow. I feel unnaturally tall. I feel hot and sticky and abused.

"Journalism at its basest is entertainment, art at its most refined. What difference does it make whether Jack the Ripper was real or made up? He's equally interesting either way. His life speaks equally to the human condition. Good fiction is often more truthful than good nonfiction.

"Take my own case. Take the case of the Bulk Mail Butcher. Does it say more about society if I'm guilty . . . or if I'm innocent? Which makes a better story: 'Editor-in-Chief Killed by Megalomaniac Food Editor with Father's Surgical Tools,' or 'Editor-in-Chief Killed by Unknown Man in a Random Act of Violence'? Which is more *perverse*? Which would make a better novel? This is how the media works and how it must.

"If you don't believe me, you need only look at the coverage. Would an instance of murder and dismemberment draw months of attention and full-scale coverage in virtually every major publication, not to mention on TV and radio, if the person killed worked in *human resources*? If the suspect were a *com-*

mon criminal? What's different about this case is that it's high-concept.

"I will grant that the method used for removing the body from the scene of the crime was novel, even spectacular. No matter who'd killed whom, the big papers would pick up that sort of thing. The question, though, is whether they'd still be interested three months after the fact. Whether the suspect would be a household name if she were not beautiful, young, and brilliant. Whether you'd be here now to hear the suspect speak.

"This is a great story for three reasons: blood, press, and power. Most would consider it sick for someone to cut up a colleague with a scalpel, no matter what the degree of precision. The fact that the players involved are magazine editors is even better, because the public loves to hate the media and the media loves to hate itself. But *power* is what matters in the end. We all wonder how far ambition could drive us, and to what extent it justifies our actions. If I am guilty as charged, you are looking at a woman willing to risk the electric chair for the sake of her career. Doesn't this make me more interesting to you? Doesn't the fact that I will *kill* for what I want make me a better interview? A better story? A greater truth is told if I'm guilty. From a journalistic standpoint, guilt is the only option."

Howard is the first to his feet. I have so much more still, but others are standing, too. What have I said? They're clapping. They're clapping for me. The sound clings to my body like static. A camera flashes and all that's before my eyes are two blue wafers, floating. Floating away.

And then we're walking. Howard leads me to the reception. He leads me by the elbow to a room that's a perfect box.

The walls, the ceiling, all the surfaces seem unnaturally flat. The fluorescent lighting doesn't improve matters. The furniture, all modern and glass and steel and leather, doesn't either.

Howard's black wingtips squeak on the tile floor. The room fills rapidly. Everybody seems to know everybody else, and soon they're all talking and drinking and whether male or female they all resemble one another: they all look like me.

Howard leaves to get me a drink. Without him at my side I'm fair game, and quickly I'm engulfed, swimming in a salad of sweatshirts and T-shirts and cotton shorts and blond, blond hair. These are the journalists of tomorrow, these members of the UCLA Journalism Society, and already they've learned to behave like a pack.

A bloated man, too old to be a student but too sloppy to be anything else, wobbles beside me. "What's the fugitive life like?" He winks, as if it's a pickup line I've not heard before.

I step back from him and still I smell his sweat. "I'm not running from anyone. It's entirely too much fun being a suspect. It helps magazine circulation." I smile. "So long as you don't end up in jail, I recommend it highly."

I see Howard. He's brought me coffee, but it doesn't matter. I take it and he grins and then he's pushed aside by a tank-topped waif with a pencil jabbed through her hair bun. "The name's Mona," she declares. "Are you guilty?"

Oddly, nobody has quite asked me this question outright, not the FBI, the press, Dmitri, Daddy. And so I'm not prepared in the usual way.

"It says here that you know too much," she persists. She unfolds an essay torn from this week's *New Republic,* one of those skeletal analyses that, with crossword-puzzle efficiency, weave clues into a grid fine enough to capture the most subtle inconsistencies. "It says you know more than you should about the details of the murder."

"It is a clever approach. I wish I'd commissioned an article like that for *Portfolio.*"

"Are you guilty, though? You haven't answered."

"I suppose I don't understand the question."

"Did you murder PJ Bullock, dismember him, and then ship his body parts across the country via UPS?"

"Yes," I say, and then smile.

She frowns. "I don't believe you."

Why should she? Lately I have the credibility of a murderer.

TWO

SAN FRANCISCO INTERNATIONAL Airport is as cultural an institution as any on the West Coast, and so exhibits are routinely mounted in the passageway from the domestic gates to the baggage check. This time it's a display of Cookware Through the Ages. Rusted medieval soup cauldrons. Watertight Hopi serving baskets. Ornate Victorian tea services. Only children ever stop to look at the display cases. When they do, their parents tell them to behave.

It's a little past ten on a Thursday morning. I'm so hungover it hurts to walk. Every pore of my face seeps sweat, although it can't be more than sixty degrees outside. My bag is heavy and I have to lean against a display of eighteenth-century French cutlery to keep from toppling.

People passing don't notice me any more than they notice the case my body obscures. A pale middle-aged woman in mink rustles by, nearly plowing over a sixty-something man in a baby-blue polyester suit with a tie ending at his bellybutton. "Excuse me," he says with some sincerity. A family of five, dressed head-to-toe in Gap, noisily passes, barely holding together at the seams. This is what it must feel like to be old. Paralyzed and invisible. I make a mental note to shoot myself on my fiftieth birthday.

On the case beside me is a copy of the *Examiner.* I don't make a habit of reading the local papers, but I do like to see if I'm featured in them. For the sake of posterity, I keep a scrapbook of clippings.

I search the pile of smudgy newsprint for the first section.

BULK MAIL BUTCHER SEXUALLY IMPOTENT
FBI RELEASES KILLER'S PROFILE

WASHINGTON—FBI officials today released a computer-generated profile describing the personality type most likely to have murdered former *Portfolio* editor PJ Bullock III. No suspects matching the profile have yet been apprehended.

"We consider this a critical breakthrough," commented Special Agent Miriam Wolfe of the forensic science unit. "We've used this technology to solve the Boston Strangler case and many others. With our new systems, we expect to compile a more extensive list of suspects and are optimistic enough to predict that we'll have the perpetrator apprehended within weeks."

The FBI, which has seen this bizarre case balloon into the biggest in recent memory, chose to employ psychological profiling despite leads on Gloria Greene that many in the media found promising. One source explained that the media has presented Greene as the only possible suspect and is conducting a trial in the press, but that the investigation from the FBI's standpoint was not limited to one suspect. Despite the frenzy around the mediagenic Greene, investigators are pursuing many different angles. Greene, who took Bullock's place as editor-in-chief of *Portfolio* shortly after his death, was unavailable for comment.

"What we're looking at," said Special Agent Wolfe at a press conference shortly after the six-page profile was released, "is a violent crime committed as an act of revenge. The damage done to the victim's body is the work of an extremely frustrated individual. We believe the perpetrator is male, between the ages of fifty and sixty, and, due to the rage of his attack, almost certainly suffers from sexual impotence."

The report also alleges that the killer is or was involved in an unsuccessful marriage and has one or more children. He was probably personally or professionally close to the victim prior to the crime, and acted out in retaliation when the victim tried to terminate the relationship.

"This was a desperate act," Special Agent Wolfe acknowledged. "We're dealing with a man who isn't psychologically stable and could act again."

Agents involved in the San Francisco investigation continue to pursue those with a medical background, particularly in anatomy or surgery, with prior connections to *Portfolio*. They anticipate that the profile will be beneficial to this effort.

"With a detailed profile, derived from an analysis

of the nature of the crime together with the methods used to commit it, law enforcement is often able to narrow or develop a list of suspects," explained UC Berkeley Professor of Criminology Frank Ametti to *Examiner* reporters. "With sufficient publicity, the technique can also be used to induce a confession."

Back in the office, Spivvy tells me I look like hell, then says I've been getting so many phone messages she stopped taking them down. I thank her with as much sarcasm as I can muster, tell her to filter my calls, and slouch back to my office with my bag drawn across my shoulder and a messy stack of While You Were Out slips in my hand.

I'm itchy with sweat in all the worst places and I'm gasping for air and can't seem to find any. I bought a cheap pair of sunglasses at LAX, because I forgot my favorite pair of Armanis back home, and I've worn them the whole trip back. I do not take them off.

Mostly it's the newspapers that have been calling, trying frantically to get a comment from the magazine. There's some TV, too, always urgent, never interested for long. And somewhere deep in the stack of messages is one from Agent Brody.

I take four aspirin from the jar in my desk, swallow them in quick progression, and, forehead propped against my hand, dial his office.

"Gloria Greene. So good to hear from you. You really should let us know when you're leaving town. I gather you've seen the news."

"You don't be*lieve* the profile, do you?"

"Do you?"

"I'll miss being the center of the investigation. The focus of your life."

"I hope you haven't planned any foreign travel."

"I have a magazine to edit."

"We may still have more questions."

"If you want to know whether I'm a fifty-year-old male doctor, the answer is no."

"Your father is. We may need some information about him."

"He's not impotent."

"He's very invested in your success." A pause. "What do you know about vecuronium bromide?"

"What should I know?"

"You should know that an inventory was just completed at your father's hospital. You should also know that vecuronium bromide has no street value. There aren't many reasons to steal it."

"First you try to build a case on circumstantial evidence against me, and now my father? He doesn't have time to be harassed." The wet of my armpits rolls down the sides of my body. "He's a very busy man. I can answer your questions. I know everything about him."

"Then you know all about Madison Olivetti, too. You and your father must have a very . . . open relationship."

"We're close. I need to go now."

"You're father's in surgery. You won't be able to reach him for over an hour."

"I *need to go*." I smack the phone down. Dial Daddy.

Dr. Greene is in surgery.

THREE

DMITRI WAKES ME BY WISHING ME A
good morning.

"What time is it?" I ask, although I can guess
the answer.

"Eleven-forty-five. I trust your dreams have been sweet."

"Um." The cheap sunglasses I bought in L.A. are wedged
deep into the flesh of my cheeks, pressed there by the weight
of my head against my desk for what must be over half an hour.

"So, where have you been all morning, Gloria?"

"My flight got in late."

"And which flight might this be?"

"From L.A. I was down there lecturing at the Journalism
Society. You remember."

"No, I don't remember, Gloria. Why do you go off lecturing in L.A. when I need you here? When I encourage you to
lecture at the schools, I don't mean you should accept invita-
tions during a criminal investigation. You leave everything for

Bruce to do, and Bruce can't understand how to run a magazine. He can't tie his shoes and walk at the same time."

"I—"

"And why are you wearing those sunglasses? You go to L.A. and now you think you're a movie star. This isn't a beach and it isn't a nightclub. This is a magazine. I'm the only one who understands this. You need to work harder."

I remove my sunglasses. Behind them, my eyes are bloodshot and wet at the lashes. Dmitri chooses not to notice.

"How am I supposed to rely on you, Gloria? You're away all the time."

"Do I sense jealousy?"

"You're stuck up, Gloria, that's your problem. And you don't fucking listen to me. I have every newspaper and TV station writing things about my magazine, and you're not here to keep track. You asked to be the one who talks to reporters and nobody else was to say anything and I told you fine, it's your thing. But you're not around when they call and Spivvy doesn't know where you are because you never tell anyone. From now on, Gloria, anywhere you go, you get permission from me first."

I roll my eyes and remove a nail file from my purse. "And if I don't, what are you going to do? Fire me?"

"Don't tempt me. You're too aloof, Gloria. Magazine sales are down almost twenty percent since you became editor. No matter what the publicity, we get newsstand returns, and people aren't renewing their subscriptions. The articles you commission, they're meaningless to our readers. Nobody cares that Martin Heidegger is the latest guru of office management consultants. Our audience wants big stars. They want Lydia Beck. This magazine is not an intellectual exercise. It's not about proving to readers that you're smarter than them, or sharing with them your latest reading list. Because they really don't care, Gloria."

"They're losers. We don't need them. Those who matter will always read *Portfolio.* They'll read it because of me. You can't get rid of me, Dmitri." But he's not looking at me now. He's toying with my Rolodex, spinning the cards so fast I can feel the breeze against my blouse. Dmitri's not paying attention, and that's intolerable. "I'm irreplaceable and you know it."

"There are always others," he reasons, stepping back.

"Bruce? Katherine? Jake? Or maybe Will O'Shaughnessy wants to come out of retirement. Shall we give him a call?" I lift my phone receiver. "Or perhaps we can . . . resurrect PJ. Too bad he'd be missing a thigh."

"Enough."

"I'm famous, Dmitri. A fucking folk hero." I return my sunglasses to my face. "A movie star. I honestly don't know what you'd do without me."

"And when your movie stops playing? What happens to you then?"

Spivvy pages me. She says it's my doctor.

"Is that you, princess?" Daddy, of course. "I can't imagine why you're worried over that Brody gentleman. He just came to the hospital again. We discussed everything. His medical background is weak."

"You didn't tell me. You didn't ask."

"We both agreed you're not a very good suspect for him. I showed him around and he thinks I'm much more suitable. I'm trying to help you. I've not had so much fun since they tried to toss me from med school. You should come here more often. Why don't you visit me at the hospital anymore? Will you come see me in prison?"

"Fuck." Sometimes Daddy acts so generous. I guess he knows he could never go to jail.

"I'm in an important meeting, but thank you for your concern and have a nice day."

"I love you, princ—"

"That was a subscriber," I inform Dmitri. "He says he *loves* the magazine. He says he loves *me*."

FOUR

EVERYTHING IS SO MUCH MORE COM-
plicated now. I used to visit Daddy at the hospital
constantly.

When I imagine him, it's always there, even if in appearance it's everything he's not. That sterile blue universe, as con-
tained as a gelatin capsule, is his domain. He moves in it with
the authority of a U.S. senator and the efficiency of a British
nanny, all latex and fresh cotton. His office is as he likes things
to be: hardwood floors covered in a patchwork of worn rugs,
Brillo-gray etchings of old men and older buildings. It's the office of a gentleman scholar, and he looks somewhat ridiculous
in it with his strong hands and sharp warm eyes.

Over time they got to know me at the hospital, the nurses
and the rest. But they seemed collectively to believe that to
greet me would be unprofessional, so instead they generally ig-
nored me. This suited me well. Like Daddy, I couldn't imagine
they had anything interesting to say.

Daddy was usually engaged in some procedure involving open incisions and peeled-back flesh when I arrived, so I'd amuse myself by sorting through pharmaceuticals in the storage closet. Of course the door was kept locked, what with all the nurses and orderlies passing through, but Daddy had long before given me the code to open it in case I ever needed anything while he was occupied.

Norcuron, lately the FBI's obsession, is packed, as any surgeon can tell you, in boxes of ten vials, each vial containing 10 mg of vecuronium bromide. Syringes are packaged fifty to a box, plastic and disposable like party favors. Scalpels are stored bladeless in a sterilizing tray, blades scalpelless in a box of their own. Latex gloves are dispensed from a carton like Kleenex. One size fits all.

Usually by the time I was through in the closet, Daddy would be waiting for me by the nurses' station, still in scrub. When he knew I was around, he tended to rush through what remained of the face he was lifting. His own interpretation of triage.

"Where have you been?" he'd ask me, slightly suspicious that I'd stolen something from the supply closet, even something as arcane as Norcuron.

"You were taking for*ever.*"

Then he'd ask whether I wanted to have lunch with him, place of my choice, his treat. Inevitably, I'd smile and nod. He'd rush off to change to his street clothes.

FIVE

PAUL GREY SITS ACROSS FROM ME,
together with his wife. We're at the Quartier Latin
Wine Bar, which is actually nowhere near the
Quartier Latin. It's in Hayes Valley, which everybody says is
the new place to be seen in San Francisco, but which still
largely resembles the dump it was before it became trendy.

I'm expensing our drinks because Paul and I went to college together and haven't seen each other in over three years,
but mostly it's that Paul does public relations. There's no separation between business and pleasure in the world of magazine
publishing. Sometimes my life feels like one big tax write-off.
Other times it feels like forced labor.

Paul's wife is brand-new, and so he twists his wedding
band around his finger while we talk. She's from Rhode Island.
Her name is Claire. She watches him suspiciously and sips her
white Bordeaux.

Claire's dress is light cotton, and through it I can see the shadow of her body. Before I can ask Paul the first thing about relating to the public, she starts talking about their trip to Napa.

"It's called the wine country because that's where they grow grapes for Chardonnay, Cabernet Sauvignon . . ."

"Gloria knows, Claire. She lives here."

"But maybe she hasn't been on the same tours we were." She turns to me. "Did you know that cork is a renewable resource?"

"Yes."

"Then you spend a lot of time in Napa."

"To be honest, I can't fucking stand Napa. I can't stand the entire state of California. Do you have any idea how dull it is being the only one on your block who gets the Sotheby's catalogues by subscription?"

Paul rattles his pager as if trying to find the toy in a Cracker Jack box. "I think I'd better return this one, honey." He stands. We both glare at him but he only winks at me.

"I don't see why Paul needs to be on the phone so often. He gets annoyed if I listen."

"He was the same way when we were together. How long have you been married now?"

"Seven months this Tuesday," she answers automatically, but she's staring at me and it's obvious he never told her. "He used the phone a lot when you two were together . . . in school?"

"It was when we were in school that we were together, if that's what you're asking. Together and then not together and then together again. He wasn't exactly what you'd call reliable." I sip my wine. "I can't imagine why he'd get married."

"He married me."

"You have a strong grasp of the obvious, Claire. It must be why he finds you so attractive."

"Were you always . . . like you are now? I can't imagine Paul dating a criminal."

"Criminal?" The word has such a thrill sometimes, like sugar granules on the tongue.

"It's what we read in the papers. It's what Paul tells me."

"Paul was a criminal, too," I reply. We liked to steal tulips from the campus flower beds for my dorm room. We used old sewing scissors, and when that didn't work we uprooted the flowers and snapped the stems in half. Since my room was big, it often took several dozen to fill it. "Paul and I were *partners* in crime."

But Paul is back already, folding into his chair, dropping a notepad into his blazer pocket.

"Did you have a nice phone call, honey?" Claire smiles viciously. "Gloria was telling me *all* about your college days."

"Well, I did leave out some of the more violent sex."

"Gloria was saying that you broke the law in college. That the two of you did together."

Before I can elaborate to exact my revenge for Paul's telephone break, a waitress appears. She has my coloring and my hair. She's not unattractive. Paul notices her, too.

Claire orders. I order. Paul stares. I order for Paul. Claire stares at me.

When the waitress leaves, Claire announces she's planning a trip to the ladies' room. I tell her to have a good time. She hesitates. Sees that I'm not coming with her and Paul's not watching. Purse strap in fist, she scoots out her chair and leaves.

"You never told your wife about your stint with me."

"I'm sure you were careful to correct my oversight."

"You were on the phone, Paul. You left me with her."

"A client called."

I press my toes against his foot. "Maybe I want to be your client, too." I stroke the top of his shoe.

"My client?"

"People are spreading rumors about me. That I may be innocent. You see the difficulty."

"I've never done PR for a suspected murderer." He smiles.

"Circulation's down nearly twenty percent now and falling. If Dmitri can be trusted."

"What you probably need are more celebrities, which I'm happy to provide free of charge."

"I don't want more fucking celebrities. That's not what *Portfolio* is about. Now that I'm in charge."

"But without celebrity—"

"I don't need to be told how to edit my fucking magazine." Paul's foot slips away. "I'm sorry. It's just that everybody's always saying *celebrity* and they don't understand. They don't see that what I'm attempting is different."

"You want to be *The Algonquin. The Algonquin* loses money, Gloria. It will always lose money. If it weren't supported by Art Reingold's schlock newspaper chain, it wouldn't exist."

"This is different, Paul." I've found his foot. Behind the leg of his chair. "I'm the editor. The celebrity is *me.*"

"You haven't been in a major newspaper all week."

"And that's precisely the problem. That's why I need you, Paul. Nobody's taking me seriously as a suspect. They're interviewing my father now, but nobody wants to talk to me. And if nobody wants to interview me, who's going to want to read my magazine? I overheard Dmitri making negative comments about the latest issue. To one of the fucking interns. He's really getting sloppy."

"Nobody can be a suspect forever, Gloria. Eventually people are going to decide you're innocent or guilty and they'll lose interest, and then you might as well wait for your obituary. You should be relieved that the FBI didn't take all those little coincidences, add them up, and actually go to trial with them. It could still happen."

"You're not helping."

"Either way, Glor, your reputation rests on the success or failure of *Portfolio*. Find a pinch suspect. Somebody expendable. Not your father. Then concentrate on high-profile articles. Maybe not all celebrities, but big stories. Bigger than Heideggerian office management. Maybe even a story that comes out of the investigation itself. You need to find what your audience wants."

"How?"

"Ask them. Because these days even I can't get through an entire issue. And I *like* you."

"But not enough to make you read my magazine. What if Claire edited it? Would you read it then?"

"God, no."

"But you love her. You find her . . . interesting."

"Not as an editor. With a magazine, that's not what matters."

"Then what attracts you to Claire?" Claire is nothing like me. She's nothing like either of us. All curves and breasts, she's the sort of woman who fills in the holes at parties, and who always goes home with someone else's boyfriend. She's not the type one expects to see married, except maybe in middle age and in the context of children and a Volvo station wagon.

"What attracts you to her?" and suddenly that's the most important thing in the world because if I know that then I'll know why people's attraction to me is slipping. Slipping away.

"Her money."

"And her tits?" Can Daddy help me after all?

"You know you look good on TV. Large breasts make a woman seem fat. If nothing else, you'll always have that going for you."

"So I'm right. It is the tits. Why *money*, though? I'd forgotten how fucking greedy you are."

"My mother thought I should."

"Your mother likes her."

"Love at first sight."

"She always hated me."

"That's because she thought you were too bright."

"And Jewish."

"That never came up."

"What do you two talk about? What do you do together? Is she as good a fuck as I was?" I look at him hard as I say this. I pull his hand to my leg. I can feel the cold of his wedding band pass through my stocking. I guide his fingers to my crotch. How easily the old motions return.

"You were the one who was unfaithful."

"I'm *always* faithful, Paul." I see Claire returning, and then Paul does and his hand slips away. "I'm faithful to me."

RATHER THAN TAKING INDIVIDUAL BASKETS to carry our groceries around, Emily and I share a cart. She's complaining to me about her mousetraps, about how no matter what she baits them with, they never catch anything. She's not sure how many mice are living with her. Her landlord wants a head count.

"What have you been using for bait? Cheese?"

"I tried pine nuts for a while, although I nearly lost a finger trying to glue them in place. You'd think they'd like pine nuts better than whatever it is my neighbors serve them."

We come around the corner into the second aisle. I take a jar of cornichons. Emily selects some Niçoise olives. In college she was notoriously bulimic. She spent most of her evenings crouched over the toilet, her finger deep down her throat, her mouth always sour and burned. She found a way to read while throwing up; her studies didn't suffer. But surely her boyfriends must have, tasting that residue of regurgitated food and stomach acid that seemed always to be on her breath. She's no longer so thin. Now she eats as I do: unhealthily.

Fortunately, Deirdre's the same way, and so when we all have brunch together it doesn't matter who orders what. Sharing food is a kind of intimacy. People in a crowd hear the same sounds and mostly see the same things. But taste isn't in the open like that. Taste is confined to the mouth, to the body's inside. In college, Emily hated me a little because I ate anything I wanted, and I could. I didn't need to be intimate with anyone then. Outside, we require each other more, Emily, Deirdre, and I. How easy it is for undesirable personalities to wear on your own until all is eroded except textbook human nature and a compendium of popular affectations collected cross-culturally and lived with a method actor's seriousness of purpose. Emily and Deirdre provide a buffer, a means of triangulating my own personality. When I relate to Emily and Deirdre, when we eat the same food or share the same shopping cart, I relate to me.

◆ ◆ ◆

While we look at produce together, I tell Emily the latest installment in the Perry Nash saga. Before I left for L.A., he was already obsessed with seeing me:

"How about the Thursday after next at eight-forty-five?"

"Don't you have a wife and children to worry about?"

"They've managed before without me."

"So have I."

Now he's begun spying on me, as well. He stalks me sometimes, and when he does I take him where I like. Follow the leader. I bring him shopping with me. I try on everything. He shakes his head when an outfit doesn't look right or fit well. He's all right that way. I'm almost coming to rely on him.

But then he always ruins the fun by talking. He catches up on the escalator. He asks whether I'd like coffee and I say no and he asks why not. This isn't part of the game.

Emily wants to know what he looks like. She's filling a bag with mixed baby greens. She picks out the arugula with her tongs.

"He's over there. By the soup display," I say, pointing the direction with my chin.

"*That's* Perry?"

"Is something the matter?"

"He's cute, Glor. Why don't you just go out with him? *I* would."

Perry has briefly vanished. He reappears in the dairy section.

"Don't you think he looks a little sinister, though?"

"Not really."

"You don't think he might be a psychopathic killer?"

"I guess anybody could be. A psychopath, that is." She looks at me. "Is he one?"

I shrug. "Have you tried peanut butter? For your mouse problem? I hear rodents find it irresistible, at least the American ones do."

We scan the shelves. There are no fewer than seventeen varieties to choose from.

She glances at me. I've not eaten the stuff since third grade. "Maybe we can ask someone who works here."

"That's an awful lot of trouble to go through for rodents," she responds. "We can figure it out ourselves, I'm sure. Don't you know anything about spreads or condiments?"

I don't, but I do know about information management. I know how to accentuate the element of truth most salient to any given situation to avoid sullying it with confusing details that might lead people to less favorable conclusions. We all do this, and when we don't, we're being dull, which is even more intolerable than wholesale lying. I present Emily with a small tub of Skippy. "It has the lowest salt content."

She nods but doesn't hear me. She's reading the label on some sleeping pills, her lips moving as if in prayer, her long fingernails bitch red against the yellow-and-white box. Do mice even eat sleeping pills? Does it take a lot for them to OD? I choose not to voice these questions, if only because I'll be the one stuck doing the research.

Once Perry has left the toiletries section for household wares, Emily and I turn the aisle. Our cart is still nearly empty, although she's added three bottles of sleeping pills. To add more bulk, I buy a couple of boxes of Kleenex. I rarely have need for Kleenex, but am perpetually buying it to look more efficient. My closets are filled with it. Someday I'll have to donate it to Goodwill.

While I look for my brand of tampons, I ask Emily how she expects to get her mice to eat the sleeping pills.

"The *mice* to eat the sleeping pills? What have the mice got to do with it? The sleeping pills are for *me.*"

"You're suicidal because you have a fucking mouse infestation?"

"Suicidal?"

"The sleeping pills . . ."

"They're for in*som*nia, Gloria. I have a bit of insomnia and I decided to get pills to help. You do realize people take sleeping pills for reasons other than to kill themselves."

"Why would *you* have insomnia? If anyone should be taking sleeping pills, it's me."

"Investigation?" she intones.

"They're blaming Daddy, as if he could actually kill some-one. And sales are down. It's all totally unjust. Perry Nash could be a psychotic with a thing for postmortem mutilation, and the FBI would never even notice. I could commit murder and my father would go to jail."

SEVEN

DADDY SAYS I REALLY SHOULD HIRE Madison Olivetti as a marketing consultant, and I'm inclined to agree. Mostly it's a matter of appearances. Her eyes are framed by thick plastic glasses fashioned to resemble the latest in thrift-shop chic. Her clothing is a stark palette of black and white, stiff and angular against her fine oval features. It's clear she's a snob because when she walks it's as if she's naked and alone.

Of course there's also the fact that Daddy's fucking Madison. At first he wouldn't tell me and I had to confront him with what the FBI said. Then he gave me the details. That she's always so accommodating. That she's usually flexible on the surgical table. That she's a professional pollster with a background in multivariable sampling, responsible for matching up unpopular candidates to popular issues in no fewer than five successful statewide campaigns. That she can do the same for *Portfolio.*

Like so many of Daddy's relationships, it started out as a

patient consultation. Madison's mother is one of Daddy's best clients, a repeat customer who likes to have the silicone re-arranged in her body as often as she likes to have the furniture moved around in her living room. It's a question of fashion, and really her seasonal alteration of her physique puts her as far ahead of her time as Lizzie Borden was ahead of hers.

Madison is somewhat more conventional. She made an ap-pointment with Daddy shortly after her twenty-fifth birthday. She came with a gift certificate from her mother good for the operation of her choice. Apparently she chose Daddy over the operating table, though, in my opinion a mistake when you consider the prominence of her nose. Daddy's usually more meticulous than that, but he does go through phases. I'm the only woman I know who's not ultimately had to surrender her surgical virginity to him.

Daddy wants Madison to work at *Portfolio* because he be-lieves in nepotism. I need Madison to work at *Portfolio* because I don't. It's essential that I be in a position to counter Daddy's more rash decisions. Our relationship depends on it.

GLORIA: Shall we begin by having you explain why you're un-employed?

APPLICANT: I'm not unemployed, Ms. Greene. As any real jour-nalist knows, this is the off-season.

GLORIA: And all your candidates lost.

APPLICANT: Some were victorious.

GLORIA: But you can't handle the responsibility of working in the state insurance commissioner's office?

APPLICANT: She's the one who wasn't reelected.

GLORIA: You're telling me you couldn't keep an incumbent in-surance commissioner in office?

APPLICANT: I don't lose, Ms. Greene. She lost that campaign for herself. If you'd been reading the newspaper before you offed your editor-in-chief, you'd know that she had an affair with the mayor of Tiburon while he was still married to the former lieutenant governor.

GLORIA: Are you accusing me of murdering PJ?

APPLICANT: To be accurate, two out of every three subscribers hold that opinion. They believe the FBI isn't doing its job.

GLORIA: And you believe them?

APPLICANT: It doesn't matter what I believe. I can help you, Ms. Greene. I can save you.

GLORIA: By setting me up with the mayor of Tiburon?

APPLICANT: By telling you that only one out of every ten gives the magazine a 'satisfactory' rating.

GLORIA: And why should I trust your methods?

APPLICANT: Three out of every ten think you should resign because of your involvement in the investigation.

GLORIA: Why should I trust your numbers?

APPLICANT: Seven out of every ten would rather have another editor if it meant the magazine was more like what it used to be. Four out of every ten believe it's slipping because you're spending more time on TV and in the newspapers than on the job.

GLORIA: Why should I believe you?

APPLICANT: Even your father doesn't like what you've done to *Portfolio.*

But that just proves Madison's information isn't entirely scientific. Daddy likes everything I do. He buys me art whenever I do something brilliant. He buys me art when we travel to Manhattan together.

My Miró is a case in point. We bought it at Christie's when I was appointed editor-in-chief of my college magazine. Daddy said we were in New York to visit my grandmother, but of course that was just an excuse. Old people get tiresome quickly, and are best left in the suburbs with their air conditioning.

Manhattan was made for people like Daddy and me. A place to go shopping for antiques and to see the museums and to eat cheeseburger deluxes for lunch. New York makes me feel romantic. I like to take Daddy for long walks through Central Park. Sometimes I make him stop and I just hug him for minutes at a time. I don't have to say much to my father because we always share the same thoughts.

The day we found the Miró, they were also showing late-nineteenth-century Russian jewelry. I tried on the most expensive pieces. Daddy made me pose so he could admire me. Other men admired me, too, and said things until Daddy got cranky and told me to meet him in the main gallery when I was done.

There were other pieces I wanted to wear, and I did. I smiled at the woman behind the counter when I pointed out what I desired and she smiled back when she laid it on the countertop. With antique jewelry, the thrill isn't so much in the history as in the fact that you can buy it.

Daddy was scowling at an awful Matisse when I found him in the main gallery. I could tell by looking in his briefcase that he'd bought me the catalogue for the Russian jewelry auction as well as the one for modern and contemporary prints.

"Where do you think you've been?"

"Is something wrong, Daddy?" I brought my body up to his and draped my arms around his neck like a tennis sweater.

He turned, lifting away my hands. "It's all a game, isn't it?"

"What do you mean?"

"You don't care. Art, jewelry, it's all the same, right? What matters is that it's expensive and that you succeed in getting me to buy it for you."

"I was having *fun* in there, Daddy. I like to try things on. You know that."

He shrugged. "Why don't you pick out a suitable print, then, and we can be on our way."

My father went to the auction alone because I insisted. I stayed at home with my grandmother and bid by phone, first against the pack, eventually against just him. I suspect we both wanted to know just how much he loved me, precisely how many dollars and how many cents I was worth to him. As a doctor, Daddy taught me to be scientific.

Later he talked about the vicious competition he'd had to fight off. He despised phone bidders. They were always at their worst when he wanted to buy.

At auction I learned the value of things. At auction I learned all I needed to know to manage a major magazine.

GLORIA: Who are your favorite artists?

APPLICANT: Nearly three-quarters of all Americans, if you must know, prefer blue landscapes. I'm a pollster, Ms. Greene. Your current ratings make Adlai Stevenson look popular. I'm only willing to take this job because your father asked as a special favor—and as you know, it's very difficult to turn down Daddy.

GLORIA: I'm not running for office, you realize.

APPLICANT: Your magazine is, though. And every issue it's losing the election to *Vanity Fair, Interview, Entertainment Weekly.* Three-quarters of your readers would like to hear about a high-stakes mountaineering expedition.

GLORIA: It's already been done. By many other magazines.

APPLICANT: Why do you think politicians all repeat one another?

GLORIA: How would my readership respond to a murder story?

APPLICANT: Reasonably well. If it ended with a confession.

GLORIA: And one about an affair between a prominent surgeon and a hack political pollster no older than his daughter?

APPLICANT: It's better than anything you've run recently. An element is missing, though. Something out of the soaps. Like that the daughter is in love with the father, too. But the pollster emerges victorious. The pollster, Gloria, *always* emerges victorious.

I hire Madison, even if for Daddy she's just a fling. He says it has to do with the seasons and surely I can understand by now that he prefers brunettes in the winter. Daddy says I shouldn't be jealous. I'm his daughter. Blood is thicker than semen.

All of which might be acceptable were he not allowing Madison to pick up the phone when she's over. She answers by saying, "Dr. Greene's residence." Of course I always hang up.

Sometimes I think Daddy doesn't realize he's being so cruel to his daughter. I forgive him because he's a doctor who has a lot to think about, medically speaking, and now the FBI is wasting his precious time. But then I want to talk to him and some woman is at his house, answering his phone as if he belonged to her and I belonged to nobody, had no father at all, and was a nuisance rather than the only person who will ever appreciate him as he ought to be appreciated.

For the sake of revenge, I've had Don Richard record my answering machine message. I tell Daddy I might get engaged.

EIGHT

SO NOW WE HAVE THE FBI SORTING through our slush pile. I hand over a stack of rejection letters to stuff the SASEs with as they go, but they're taking their task seriously and only Brody smiles at me.

They're being ridiculous and they know it, but appearing attentive to detail is critical in the law enforcement business. A week or so back, an intern at *L.A. Transfer* went to the hospital after sending out a large group of rejection letters. They pumped his stomach and found he'd ingested a dose of arsenic. It was only a matter of time before a writer, tired of rejection, started poisoning the glue on his SASEs to kill off the people turning down his manuscripts.

It was pure Darwinism, really, like any sensible crime.

Soon after, *Transfer* received a letter warning of the perils of hasty rejection. We were sent one, too, a poorly Xeroxed warning written on a typewriter with clogged p's and q's. It was signed, "The Bulk Mail Butcher."

The magazine world is like that, though, which is something those outside it can't understand. Writers are unstable people; that's why they write. Editing can be a dangerous profession, and anybody who licks envelopes deserves to get killed.

Emmett gives me a strange, annoyed look when I tell him this. He is presiding over an elaborate operation, involving titration and other procedures I've tried to forget since college. They've taken over the entire mailroom, turned it into a crime lab. This is the sort of thing you expect the FBI to do when they're investigating a murder, and the only reason Brody and Emmett are here, the only reason anybody is, I'm sure, is for image. Out front a TV crew awaits their heroic exit.

Spivvy isn't taking it lightly. She's abandoned her post in the reception area. The rumor is she's locked herself in a bathroom stall and won't come out until the Bulk Mail Butcher is behind bars. The interns aren't in such good shape, either. They're camped out in the library, where they're fact-checking stories given to them by Dana, the research editor. The envelope scare frightened her, too, but what frightens her more is the fact that the interns, in their agitated state, are letting whole words slip by unverified.

"I don't know what to do," she says to me.

"Tell them to do their jobs or get a life."

She rolls her eyes as if I'm the one causing offense, and then brushes past me to retrieve some interview transcripts.

Rake calls me over. He's leaning against Katherine's desk, acting as if it's a national holiday, speculating on what books the Bulk Mail Butcher likes to read. Katherine's sitting on her file cabinet, arms crossed over her jumper. The scene resembles one of those impossible publicity shots you see in company prospectuses and college viewbooks.

"What do *you* think of Bret Easton Ellis, Gloria?"

"I liked *American Psycho.* I found it . . . inspirational."

I feel Agent Brody's hand on my shoulder. "I think we all did." He coughs. "May I have a word with you?"

Broken glass and liquid are spilled all over the hallway. Brody helps maneuver me through the mess, explaining that a technician with a box of labwire tripped on a manuscript.

"Did you find anything interesting in the mailroom?" I ask, trying to sound interested.

"You people get a lot of articles sent to you."

"But no poison penmanship?"

"Not yet, there isn't."

"My staff is worried." With PJ, it was somebody else's funeral. Now the killer doesn't seem so remote.

"The letter is a hoax, you know."

"I'm not foolish."

"It's all about momentum. We feel we have some."

"I can't imagine that you can't find somebody to fit your profile." I smile at him.

"Your father's good enough. For government work." He smiles back. "Even were he acquitted, there'd be little of his career to return to by the time the legal proceedings were through."

"Your own search of the hospital turned up the missing vecuronium bromide."

"The serial numbers didn't match."

"A manufacturing glitch."

"We found the batch they came from."

I told Daddy this would happen.

"They came from the hospital at UCSF."

I told him they'd eventually think of the obvious.

"Where your father once practiced."

I told him he doesn't have a mind for this.

"Where none of the door combinations have been changed."

I told him that stealing is dishonest.

"We found his fingerprints on the box."

I told him only dishonest people get caught.

"So, to answer your question, we've found somebody to fit the profile. The question is, do *you* think your father's guilty of killing PJ Bullock? Do you think he should spend his life in jail?"

"And if I don't?"

"If you believe he's innocent, Gloria, you must have a reason. You're an intelligent woman. You know better than to trust appearances when it comes to innocence and guilt. So tell me what you know. If your father didn't kill PJ, then tell me who did."

We're on the street now, in front of the office. TV crews converge on us, nosing their cameras so close they touch skin. Brody smiles. Waves. He tells me I should smile and wave, too.

"You look like a criminal," he tells me, smoothing my lapel. "Was it something I said? Or something you haven't?"

IV. DISSECTION OF THE WRIST

Divide the integument in the same manner as in the dissection of the anterior brachial region . . . The muscles will then be exposed. The removal of the fascia will be considerably facilitated by detaching it from below upward.

—GRAY'S ANATOMY

ONE

MY FATHER'S SPEEDING-TICKET-RED BMW is waiting in the neighboring driveway when I step out the door to my apartment. He's rolled back the roof. For once it's sunny and for once I'm able to wear my red paisley skirt without fussing over tights. It's eleven-thirty in the morning. It's Valentine's Day.

"How's my valentine this morning?" he asks, holding the passenger door open and helping me into the car.

I roll my eyes.

"Late night, was it?" He shuts my door, returns to his side, and gets in. He's wearing a navy blazer over a gray turtleneck, the way I like him to when we go places.

"I got you a little present, princess." He hands me a box of Godiva truffles. "I know how you like them."

The truffles are a tradition by now, as is Valentine's Day itself. Daddy and I spend it together every year, shopping for antiques and then going to dinner. When I was in college, Daddy had to fly to Massachusetts every February. He wrote it off as a business expense.

"I thought we'd spend the day in Petaluma."

I nod and bite into a chocolate. We always spend the day in Petaluma, and I always eat truffles in the car, feeding the ones I don't like to Daddy. He pretends not to notice the bite marks.

As we approach the Golden Gate Bridge, we hit Saturday morning traffic. The sun is intense, reflecting off the bay as in a bad postcard. Daddy slips a CD into the player. Nirvana. It's the disc I gave him a couple of months ago when I decided he was listening to too much Chopin.

"The traffic was lighter on the way in." He changes lanes and switches back again, honking when somebody tries to cut him off.

"Christ, Daddy."

"I hate to waste all this time."

To distract him, I ask about the medical seminar he just attended.

"Did I tell you about the new lasers?"

I shake my head. Bite into truffle.

"There's a model that cuts clear through filet mignon, princess. Used to be lucky to cleave a flank steak . . ."

"I remember."

"And the vacuums! Oh, if only you could have watched them suck and bag tubs of Jell-O . . . English trifle . . . You know, it's not too late. You could go to medical school if you ever want to leave that awful mess behind. I can get you into UCSF."

"I *like* what I'm doing. It's what I've wanted my whole life."

"We could go into practice together. You know you were always talented with a scalpel."

"I'm talented with a pen, too, Daddy. I don't see why people can't give me a fucking chance. Circulation isn't only *my* responsibility." But that's not the issue because what I want is for him to really listen to me. Too often when we talk it's as if I'm his model, and only good for the face he's projected on so many of his patients as if it were shorthand for all of me.

We eat lunch at Gene's Deli, where they wrap everything in butcher paper. There's sawdust on the floor and it works its way into my sandals, making my feet dirty, making me anxious. I can taste all the cigarettes I inadvertently smoked with Emily last night. Her cigarettes. If you never buy them yourself, you can't be an addict.

We have to wait our turn. I tell Daddy I want tuna on nine-grain and a Calistoga, and then I find the bathroom. I don't have to pee, so I end up standing in front of the mirror, retouching my lipstick.

Everything is much more pleasant when I sit down across from Daddy on the patio. He's already unwrapped my sandwich for me. He's removed the cap from my mineral water.

Daddy is having roast beef on whole wheat, blood rare, the way he likes it. His hair has gone completely silver in the last few years, and in the sun it looks like money. People always say my father resembles this or that senator, and some even think he should run for office and when they do I'm flattered. He has the narrow face and the deep-set eyes of an aristocrat. At the moment, he also has mayonnaise on his chin.

I laugh at him as I wipe it off with my napkin. "You're turning into one of those social security types who walk around all day wearing their favorite condiments on their face."

"You think I'm getting old." He frowns and I don't laugh anymore.

"You're very handsome, Daddy." I touch my index finger to his nose to reassure us both. "The most handsome man I know."

And then we're in the antique stores together and it's all trash, the jewelry and watches, although the hooded Rolex bubbleback I wear gets compliments and an offer.

Daddy finds me leaning over one of the dusty old jewelry counters and, kissing my neck, tells me to cover my eyes. "Count to three, princess." When he lets me take my hands away, I'm looking at a pair of vintage wooden skis.

"What are you going to *do* with them?" I ask. My father collects anything related to skiing. Most of it's junk, and none fits together. Fortunately, it's all stored in closets.

"Aren't they wonderful?"

"I guess."

"We should go skiing again. You still won't, will you?"

"I told you I'm in retirement."

"We had fun together."

"Daddy, I appreciated it. I don't have time."

"I never see you anymore."

"We're spending *today* together." I feel like a six-year-old. "Most of the time you're with Madison anyway. As if I weren't your fucking daughter."

"Come. There are other antique stores and it's already past four."

"Aren't you getting your skis? Although I suspect Madison prefers jewelry. She absolutely adores wearing your old wedding band at the office." An offense for which I'd fire her, were she not so unforgivably useful.

"It's not important." He pretends not to care, but he doesn't wipe my eyes when they tear, and he won't put his arm around me when I get close.

♦   ♦   ♦

Daddy and I skied all winter long when I was in high school and he wasn't married or dating anybody. To avoid the traffic to Tahoe, I'd skip Friday-afternoon classes and meet him in back of the school. He took care of everything. He got me Diet Cokes for the ride up. I did my homework while he drove.

On the slopes we were competitive. He'd learned to ski with my grandfather years before it became popular, when rope tows were the rage and grooming was accomplished by sideslipping down the mountain before skiing it. He was an East Coast skier, a snob who said I had it easy.

But I was younger and in better shape, despite my aversion to sports. I kept pace with him, even down KT-22. Daddy's legs always touched when he skied. He never fell. When I stumbled, he got angry and made me find my skis and poles on my own. That's how I learned to be a good skier. It's how I learned self-reliance.

We ate lunch late and were never down the mountain before the lifts closed because neither Daddy nor I was willing to be tired first.

"Are you hungry?"

"Not yet."

"Me either."

Lunch came only after I started falling often and Daddy insisted we take a break. We ate big burgers with onions, and bowls of chili. We drank beer.

For dinner, we had ribs sometimes, or plates of all-you-can-eat spaghetti, in dark, angular restaurants crisscrossed with heavy wooden beams. We slept in the same bed because I got cold, even with blankets and the radiator.

♦ ♦ ♦

At dinner, I tell Daddy about work and the new suspect who everyone's saying is so guilty. The restaurant is clean and white and belongs to the husband of a patient. We don't look at the menus for over an hour. We finish our first bottle of wine.

"Are you certain Perry Nash is the one?"

"He fits the psychological profile. Fits it better than you ever did."

"I really didn't mind. For you."

"I did." I lean in close. "Nobody believed it, anyway. You were on call the night of the murder. The FBI went after you for my sake, to make me confess. But of course there are other possibilities. Always others, and they didn't think of that."

"Is it what you want, though? You have given it some thought."

"You think it's sexy that I'm an accused murderess. You know, you're so preposterous sometimes." I kiss him on the cheek.

"I know how you love to be in the spotlight."

"Only for the good of the magazine. Only for the benefit of subscribers." But even Madison, who I'm sure would enjoy seeing me off to jail, says having me at the center of a criminal investigation isn't an efficient way to persuade the public to read *Portfolio.* "Wouldn't you still be proud of me if I wasn't in the papers all the time?"

"Of course I'd be proud of you, princess. No matter what." He strokes my hand under the table. "If you need me to stand trial, just say so. If you need to do it yourself, I'll give you money for new clothes."

"You don't like what I'm wearing?" I look down at my body. "You don't like the way I look?"

"Madison's clothing is always crisply ironed. I want what's best for you. You can understand that."

I attempt a weak smile. "I know." The smile withers.

"I'd do anything for you, princess."

"Would you commit murder?"

"I think you should be less judgmental about the FBI. They may be dull-witted, but I doubt it's for the reasons you think."

And then he stops because otherwise the conversation will turn serious and maybe I'll tell him things he'd rather leave to his imagination. Because otherwise it will be like seeing the movie instead of reading the book on which it's based, and overlaying an actor's looks on a character, ninety-three minutes of script on a narrative. Daddy hates the movies and so he doesn't understand why sometimes I need to be serious with him and tell the truth.

I find a waiter at my shoulder, eager for my order. I select the grilled salmon. Daddy gets the rack of lamb.

"You know all that red meat is going to kill you."

"You sound like your mother."

"God help us." Under the table, I kick my sandals away. I rest my feet on his lap.

"What did Debra think of my stint as the Bulk Mail Butcher?"

"Sidney said it explains a lot."

"And you agreed?"

"I told him you're a doctor. I said you have too much respect for the human body to treat it as junk mail."

He grasps my ankles. Thrilled. "What about your mother, though?"

"Sidney thinks you corrupted her. That's why he doesn't trust her with anything. He thinks you corrupted all of us. Made us all *meshugge*."

"His word, I'm sure."

"And Mom just fucking sits at the dining room table, nodding her head. Sidney isn't even cute."

"You know it's different for an older woman."

"You always said she was your child bride."

"You're my child bride, princess."

Daddy tries to kiss me across the table, but I pull away and sit back in my chair with my napkin stretched primly across my lap.

TWO

I DON'T CARE THAT YOU USUALLY DEAL with our distributors," I enunciate into the telephone to ensure that no number of crossed lines or language barriers can obliterate my point. "I'm the editor-in-fucking-chief. If you ever want my magazine in your shithole Seven-Eleven again—"

The store's manager, whom I've called about our latest circulation problem, interrupts to ask whether I'm the former murder suspect.

"Yes, suspect, former suspect, whatever. The point is, I will not have *Portfolio* displayed on the same rack as your fucking women's magazines. Don't lie to me. I see the racks on my way to work. Your placement is undermining our credibility. *Un-der-min-ing our cred-i-bil-ity.* Have you ever fucking read *Portfolio*? . . . Not recently? . . . Not even shoplifted in your store now? . . . Well, it's your fault, whatever the fuck your name is. I wouldn't shoplift *Portfolio,* either, if I thought it was just another *Glamour* or *Woman's Day* . . . You're not listening to *me*. Do *not* disconnect me again. I will not have my circulation fucked over by a convenience-store clerk with a fourth-grade education . . . *Fourth grade ed-u-ca-tion* . . . Hello?"

"Hello?" Somebody's standing in my doorway, staring at me. Black hair, fingernails, biker boots, all collected on a frail, sunless body. It looks familiar, somehow.

"May I help you?"

"Do you mind if I come in?" A rhetorical question apparently, as she's already crossed the threshold and is crouching into one of the chairs opposite my desk. "We need to talk."

"And you are?"

"Randy. One of your interns."

I roll my eyes, but still my words are polite. "I have some important phone calls to make, Randy, and while I appreciate your eagerness to help, there's really nothing I—"

"It's not that. I'm leaving, you see."

I lift the phone receiver, start to dial the grocery store where Emily and I shop and where *Portfolio* is displayed next to *TV Guide.* I look up and she's still there. "Then leave."

"That's not what I mean. What I mean is, leaving for good."

I shrug. "Then leave for good." I keep dialing.

"I need to be with my family. I've just tested HIV-positive."

"I'm terribly sorry. Will that be all?" And then it takes a moment for what she says to have any more meaning than the words in a magazine. Randy? Is she the former mortician's assistant from Seattle? The philosophy major at Amherst?

"My boyfriend is sorry, too."

"Boyfriend?"

"Sorry. But I'm not." She attempts to laugh. "I'm no longer a poseur. I can . . . relate."

Why is she telling me this? Why these details, and why am I the recipient? Am I so anonymous? Chilly as a confessional? Ubiquitous as a god? I look down at the circulation report as if maybe that has the answers, but of course numbers never answer anything. Numbers only question. Question authority. And still Randy is talking.

"I mean, if I get sick, it's going to suck. But at least now there's a time frame on my life. I need that. It's like, now I feel motivated."

"Um." I study the numbers and make calculations of my own: PJ didn't sleep with Randy. She wasn't Dmitri's type. Who else? Did anybody sleep with PJ who also slept with someone who slept with her? Six degrees of separation, that's all there is between us.

"My boyfriend already had it, if that's what you're wondering. I probably got it from him, not from anyone here. I never cheated much. He's all remorseful now, and that's going to fuck our relationship, but it does have some positive effects. I wanted to be closer. That's what he can't understand."

Circulation in free-fall. Editors deteriorating. Death, maybe mine, and all Randy wanted was to be close. AIDS has made sex so messy. No matter what your dexterity, condoms are ungraceful. AIDS has made sex more momentous than it was ever meant to be.

"You realize this affects more than just you," I politely remind her. "There are always others."

"I don't understand."

"I suppose you wouldn't." I pause to straighten a wayward shoulder pad. I purge all sympathetic impulses from my system because that's what it means to be editor-in-chief, to manage in spite of the emotional backwash. "Look, Randy. I don't know who you slept with in this office, but I can't afford to have editors getting AIDS and screaming for disability." My voice feels distant now. Distant the way it should be. I'm managing. Doing my job. "I have a magazine to run here. I'm under a lot of pressure, more than you or any of your sick little boyfriends." I open my desk drawer and in it I find a Mont Blanc. I pass it across the desk to her. "I want you to make a list. Make a list of everyone acquainted with *Portfolio* with whom you've had sexual contact, and what sort of protection you used. This is important. I have to plan."

"But I've—"

"You can start with Dan." The first month she was at *Portfolio,* Randy nearly lived in Dan's apartment. They didn't even bother coming to work on separate buses.

Randy stands and staggers toward the door, the pen in one hand, a sheet of *Portfolio* stationery in the other. "I don't have time for this bullshit, Randy. I've got circulation issues to worry about. You're a fucking intern. Get me that list."

THREE

EVERYBODY IN THE PLACE NOTICES who I'm sitting with, which is to say that nobody notices me. Being a perennial suspect in a gruesome murder has its advantages, but nothing in life can compete with the allure of the actress du jour.

In person, as on screen, Lydia Beck is beautiful. She's tall, built like a racehorse, and looks about as old as she is, which is seventeen. Her hair is darker than it appears in the movies, her features more subtle. She's dressed in her trademark kilt and navy riding jacket. She feeds on her nails between sentences.

"So, do you edit in pen or pencil?"

Lydia is researching a role she's to play in an upcoming movie, and my help comes in exchange for an exclusive cover, all arranged, of course, by Paul Grey. Lydia takes no notes and shows no signs of interest when I answer her questions. She's a method actress and already at work and I feel like I'm speaking into a mirror.

GLORIA: Red pen, but I don't, much. Edit, I mean. Mostly it's meetings.

LYDIA: You're like my manager, then.

GLORIA: More like a movie director. A great editor is an artist.

LYDIA: Are you a great editor?

GLORIA: I edit a great magazine.

LYDIA: Of course, everyone knows it isn't what it used to be. That must be hard.

GLORIA: Finding new audiences has its risks.

LYDIA: Like losing your original one?

GLORIA: I want articles that outlast the summer movies, that mean something on their own, that create culture rather than reflect it.

LYDIA: You want immortality.

GLORIA: I'll settle for archiving potential.

LYDIA: You want to edit *The Algonquin.*

The place we've gone is a new Chinese restaurant on Union Street, which really isn't Chinese at all but which specializes in so-called Shanghai cuisine. It is called Opium. Everybody inside, including the waiters and the chef, is Caucasian. The decorator, who's made the restaurant look like a dining car on the Orient Express, apparently is, too. The Chinese, even the old Shanghai Chinese, don't fashion restaurants like this. A fancy Chinese establishment is decorated with lots of ornate woodwork, and costumes its waiters in red polyester tuxedos. Opium is in the French bistro tradition. Everything is beautiful and clean. The food is mercifully simple. The wait, without reservations or celebrity, is up to two hours on a good day.

Lydia has been studying her menu throughout our dialogue. I'd thought it was to keep her head low, to help conceal herself from the public. I start reading my own, trying desperately to catch up.

"You don't know what you want? Being an editor, you must come here all the time."

I'm prepared to arrange some exotic version of the truth about Opium and my life, but the waiter, eager for our orders, saves me from myself. Lydia asks for the rice noodles with prawns and I have shiitake dumplings. She orders an iced tea. I have a Tsingtao. She asks me what it is, and when I tell her, she cancels her iced-tea order and asks for one, too. Falling out of character, she whispers to me that she has no tolerance.

LYDIA: It must suck, being Perry Nash's understudy and not a real murderer anymore.
GLORIA: There are advantages to Perry, you know.
LYDIA: Such as?
GLORIA: Avoiding jail.
LYDIA: But wouldn't you like to be as famous as Jeffrey Dahmer?
GLORIA: Not all of us can be.
LYDIA: But *you* could, Gloria.
GLORIA: You don't think Perry Nash is guilty?
LYDIA: As if! It was your idea, wasn't it? Good thing you're not in casting.
GLORIA: What's wrong with Perry? What's not believable?
LYDIA: Real killers have a look. Just like real celebrities. You'll have your comeback, Gloria. I believe in you.

Lydia tells me I'm exactly the way she wants her character to be. The movie is based loosely on *Crime and Punishment,* only set in the present and at a major national magazine. She wonders whether she should get her hair cut in a bob. She asks about my wardrobe. What she wants to understand is my life.

"The thing about being an editor is that it's not a nine-to-five job. When I was first an intern at *Portfolio,* I had a reputation for sleeping around. People knew what I was doing to solicit big-name writers, and they made snide remarks. But the fact was, I got those writers and I got results." The waiter has put a third beer in front of me. Lydia must have ordered another round between sentences, when I was too distracted to notice. Is it illegal to intoxicate a minor in public? "There's a stigma attached to sex and to using your body and that kind of thing, especially if you're a woman, and I just don't get it. It's another tool. Why shouldn't it be used? I'm good at what I do because I will do *any*thing to get what I need."

Lydia says she understands me. She says she feels the same way, and then her voice trails. She's hardly touched her prawns, except to squeeze their tails free with her chopsticks. She giggles. She has a hard time signing the check, which she absolutely insists on paying because she can charge it to the studio. "The best thing about being famous is that sometimes they don't bother turning in the credit slip. They'd rather have my autograph."

She leaves in a taxi, still giggling as she collapses into the slick black seat. "Look me up in LA-LA-land." Then she becomes serious. She digs around in her bag until she finds an issue of *Portfolio,* the first I edited. "Sign the cover to me, *por favor,*" she says, holding out a ballpoint. "You're going to be a star. This is just the beginning."

FOUR

A British gentleman takes as much pride in the size of his business card as an American does in the size of his cock, and that is the essential distinction between the two species," I'm explaining to one of *Portfolio*'s key advertisers, the recently knighted chairman of a large London distillery. It's *Portfolio*'s monthly release party. This time it's at Martians, a trendier-than-thou SoMa bar with alien memorabilia on the walls.

"And what is the American equivalent of gold embossing?" he asks, handing me his card.

I look down. It could as easily be an invitation to a coronation, or to a Long Island baby shower. "Latent homosexuality."

Dmitri cuts between us and I have to step on a passing waiter to accommodate his girth. He pumps the distiller's hand and guides him from me to the bar. Dmitri tugs and the man resists and I shrug and smile at the next person I see.

It's Don Richard, outfitted in an imported tweed suit and

with a martini in each hand. "Want to see what my next business card's going to look like?" I trade him for one of the drinks.

"You don't have heraldry, though." He runs a finger across the gilded edge. "Do you?"

"That's not heraldry, Don. It's plum sauce."

Really, Dmitri should have known better. This is what happens when you serve Chinese appetizers at a formal party. Usually it's pan-Asian and we don't have these problems. It's difficult enough keeping the ever-changing crowd of advertisers and writers and photographers doused in alcohol without having to worry about staining them.

"So, then we know it's six figures," I overhear one writer saying to another. They're on one of the UFO-shaped sofas with which the place is so densely populated.

"Quarter mil, I hear, plus screen option."

"How in Fucksville, U.S.A., do you turn a spoof of *Robert's Rules of Order* into a movie?"

I smile at them. They offer me some of the spring rolls they've hoarded.

"And get an option of a quarter mil when we're here starving on fucking dim sum and martinis."

"Speaking of starving, you hear about Georgia McKenzie's latest book? Infant pornography. Even the British publishers won't touch it."

"That's what happens when your agent dumps you. Word gets around, and you're fucked at the drive-through."

"To say nothing of the sell-through."

"Oh, really?" interrupts the woman next to me, turning. She's all khaki and denim. As usual, her face is without makeup and looks as washed out as a laundered five-dollar bill.

"Hello, Georgia. Spring roll?"

I leave them. Spending more than three minutes in any single conversation at a cocktail party is socially immature. I see other faces, other dots to connect in the puzzle that is my life. Mostly it's a matter of finding the true target and, like a hunter tracking birds, to misshoot by a few feet, anticipating the effects of time and space. By targeting someone next to the person you're after, you force the one you want to target you. All of which works brilliantly unless an act of nature like Dmitri plows you into a corner.

"May I be of assistance?" I ask him, breathing in his two-hundred-proof breath. Behind him I see Agent Emmett, questioning a waitress about dry vermouth.

Dmitri points a fried wonton at me. I watch a drop of sweet-and-sour sauce spatter one of his patent leather shoes. He's wearing his tux. I dip my napkin into my martini and try to wipe a Rorschach of soy sauce from his shirt.

"Stop that. Now." Dmitri puts my hand at my side. He takes my martini from me and drops the wonton in the glass.

"What do you want, Dmitri? There are guests."

"There won't be soon if you keep up this behavior, Gloria." He edges me farther into the corner, makes me smaller until I feel like I'm in a Herb Ritts photo. "Sir Philip is not a fucking homosexual."

"Who's Sir Philip?"

"Sir Philip is a friend of ours. An advertiser. He owns the company responsible for the alcohol you're so enthusiastically endorsing with your drinking tonight."

"Then why'd you put a fried wonton in it? If I were Sir Philip, I'd be more offended by that than I would by hearing—"

"You offend our advertisers, Gloria." Dmitri stomps his

foot. By carefully reaching past his stomach, I'm able to retrieve another drink from a passing tray. "You offend our advertisers and then they go away."

"Your tie is crooked, Dmitri. You look foolish." I sip and then I feel better but it's never enough, not with Dmitri and his wonton and his soy-stained shirt.

Rake approaches. He puts a hand on Dmitri's shoulder. Grins. "May I cut in?"

"Gloria and I aren't through. Go away. Leave us alone." He wags the martini glass as he speaks, and the wonton bobs up and down in Sir Philip's gin.

"No, thanks. I just ate."

Dmitri waits for Rake to leave. "You need to fire him, Gloria. He doesn't know how to stay out of other people's business."

"Rake's just friendly, Dmitri. Something you'd never understand. Are we done now? Did you bring me any Cuban cigars?"

"Maybe you're right. Maybe I should terminate you instead."

"Whatever for?"

"The way you're running my magazine, I have to fire someone. I can't support an editorial staff of seven with a distribution no bigger than . . . your tolerance. And now you bring the FBI to our launch party. If not for you, they wouldn't be here, making our advertisers nervous. You ruin my event."

"You always fucking exaggerate. It grows tiresome, Dmitri. Why don't you pick on one of your precious advertisers?"

"What am I supposed to tell them? We print 500,000 magazines but we distribute only fifty?"

"Fifty thousand?"

"Fifty copies. Now that Seven-Eleven's suspended orders indefinitely."

"Suspended?"

"Indefinitely."

"Whatever for?"

"A franchisee was verbally abused about his placement of the magazine. He says the editor-in-chief made crude and inappropriate comments over the telephone."

I shrug. "Fuck the Seven-Eleven clerk."

"He owns twenty franchises in California. The president of the company is a golfing partner."

"Then fuck Seven-Eleven." I've never much cared for Slurpees and I can't imagine our target reader does either.

"This is serious, Gloria."

"At least I don't have soy sauce on my shirt."

"Stop switching the fucking topic. With PJ, advertisers asked that advance copies of *Portfolio* be overnighted to them so they could show off to their friends. Now they don't even notice who's on the cover."

"Nobody ever went broke underestimating the intelligence of the American advertiser." When in doubt, misquote Mencken. And drink more martinis.

"You're pathetic, Gloria."

"I'm not a sixty-year-old serial bachelor. I'm not fat or bald."

"You're fired, Gloria."

"No, I'm not." Smiling.

"Meaning what?" Confused.

"I'm your greatest asset. Now give me a cigar."

"Look at you." He stumbles forward. I step back: cat and mouse. "You wiggle your ass and it's like you own the world. You take nothing seriously."

"And what specifically does the position of my ass relative to the world have to do with my competence as an editor? If anything, I thought people around here saw my ass as company property." I bite deep into an olive and feel the toothpick splinter between my teeth. I drop my martini glass to the floor and step down. Hard. "Or would you like to trade it in for PJ's severed cock?"

"I let you get away with many things, Gloria." Dmitri's so close he's nearly speaking into my mouth. "I don't ask questions. But you have my warning now. The next issue sells every fucking copy. I don't care what you do. You make me a miracle. Or you make yourself a new career."

Dmitri stares at me and says nothing and then I realize he's too drunk to continue, no longer even listening. I check his breast pocket for cigars and, finding none, I kick him in the shin and tell him to move. I point him in the direction of the bar.

People cling to me like warm socks. When they become tiresome I yawn and turn away. I introduce writers to photographers and photographers to advertisers and sometimes I introduce the same people twice but it's okay because nobody remembers. There's music. Live and jazz and it's in one corner far from the bar which is where everyone wants to be. People ask me questions. I smile and shrug. I point to the music. I fill my mouth with slabs of Peking duck. I drink martinis.

"How's life as a non-suspect? . . . Haven't seen you in the papers lately . . . Is it true about cancellations? . . . Are you really thinking of leaving the business? . . . People say you're being pushed out, but *I* don't believe it . . . Who will I pitch my articles to, now?"

Madison motions me over. Her face is overcrowded with

makeup. Her heels make her taller than me. She has to bend slightly to meet my ear, so that she can be heard over the conversational static. Hands against knees. I watch her veins rush bloodied alcohol through her arms.

"I want you to meet *Al*bert." I grasp his hand while she explains to me that he's a pollster in Vancouver, visiting for the week.

"That must be an easy job."

"And why?" Albert asks me.

"Nobody in Canada has an opinion. It's like asking lima beans their favorite color."

"Gloria is the editor of *Portfolio*," Madison interrupts. "She's the one who hired me to fix the magazine."

"I didn't hire you to fix anything," I remind her for what must be the hundredth time this week. I turn back to Albert, who maybe because of the lima beans won't make eye contact. "I hired her to monitor the changing tastes of our readers."

"So that Gloria can more effectively subvert them with her content."

"Your polling results aren't meaningful enough to subvert anything, except for your credibility."

"Mostly because you don't have enough readers left for me to do a scientific sampling."

"So now you've been talking numbers with Dmitri? Behind my back?"

"Everybody knows—" She looks at Albert, whose head swivels to and fro as if he were watching a tennis match.

"Nobody knows anything unless I tell them. You're a fucking pollster. We could be up for a Pulitzer and you wouldn't know."

"We are?"

"We will be. And the rumors about me leaving, maybe they're true."

"Leaving?" Agent Brody has joined us.

"A successful editor is *always* in demand."

Madison snorts. Guides Albert by the arm away to an open table. "Looks like she murdered another one," I hear her mutter, but with Canadians there's no point because they lack a sense of humor about such things. Like asking lima beans their favorite knock-knock joke.

"All that and a Pulitzer too?" Brody persists.

"Now that I actually have time to do my job, anything's possible. Speaking of jobs, have you thrown Perry Nash in jail yet?"

"You'll be the first to know." He guides me away from the crowd, back to the corner where Dmitri interrogated me, still crackly with glass. He turns my way and tries to look stern and he does, or at least as stern as is possible when your head is big and round like a golf ball at tee-time. "You need to tell me more, Gloria. More about Perry's fighting with PJ, more about their relationship. You can't keep avoiding my phone calls. We have no physical evidence against him, and the only motive is that PJ rejected one of his articles. We can't continue investigating unless there's progress. We'll get massacred in the media."

"Massacred?"

"You look better on TV."

"I'm more attractive."

"And who doesn't like a story about murdering the boss and taking his place? People think you're living the American dream while we're busy following hocus-pocus computer profiles—"

"Generated on equipment," I add for dramatic effect, "that cost taxpayers countless millions with minimal impact on crime thus far. Which will surely be taken into consideration when Congress considers funding next year."

"We believe in finding the right suspect."

"From the standpoint of PR."

"From the standpoint of justice."

"You're really of no use to me anymore. My pollster says circulation won't benefit from my continued involvement as a suspect, and my publicity consultant would rather that I not be in the papers so much. Overexposure, you know."

"Have you retained an attorney?"

"An attorney? You have no physical evidence against me except a telephone calling card I was using as a bookmark, the absence of two Norcuron vials from my father's hospital, later turned up, albeit with mismatched serial numbers, and a broken clavicle—which are a dime a dozen, given their fragility. And poor Rake and Don Richard have been disturbed about my alibi how many times?"

"People's memories are faulty, Gloria."

"Not about a night like that." From a tall china-doll waitress I take two more martinis. I hand one to Agent Brody. He shakes his head but then he takes it anyway, and chews on the olive. "To our deaths!" I smile. Glass against glass. The alcohol flows across my tongue with the familiarity of an old friend.

"Sometimes alibis are too memorable. Too memorable to be anything but staged."

"Ah, you must mean the alibis of murderesses who are too guilty. Too guilty to be anything but free."

FIVE

EVEN IF PJ HAD SURVIVED THE NIGHT, people would have remembered my evening with Rake and Don Richard. Alibis have always come easy to me. I am not an easy woman to forget. It's only natural that Rake and Don Richard remembered all the details.

They were planning to have a couple of drinks after work. Would I come along? I said yes because with all the noise and people around the office, I couldn't get a thing done. I'd been out with Rake and Don Richard before. They both drank as if Prohibition had never ended. And they played darts.

To Rake and Don Richard, darts wasn't a game. It was an ongoing series of battles, second only in importance in the history of the United States to the Revolutionary War. I never needed to pay for my drinks when I went out with them, since their personal bylaws required that the vanquished pick up the tab. I've never seen the point in arguing over personal bylaws, even if they apply to a game favored by children and drunks.

As usual, they'd chosen an obscure bar halfway across the city for that night's tournament. In the Yellow Pages it boasted *Championship Facilities—All Regulation.* They all said this, the bars Rake and Don Richard frequented, and yet they were never satisfied. Inevitably the one who lost would find some way to fault the setup, the atmosphere, the ill-conditioned ale.

The pub, a place in the Inner Sunset called Osgood's, was virtually empty when we arrived. From somewhere could be heard the brassy sound of a small transistor radio, tuned to one of those newstalk stations all transistor radios are hard-wired to receive. Aside from that, cavernous silence.

Before we could order, Don and Rake investigated the darts setup. According to their personal bylaws, both had to agree to its suitability before engaging in a tournament or buying any alcohol. "All regulation," the bartender offered. "And we've a selection of darts you can choose from."

Rake waved him off. Both had their own darts, which they kept in tight leather pouches that looked like chocolate bars. Don Richard, meanwhile, was pacing off the distance to the board. He nodded. Rake nodded back.

"Can we please have just one pint before you start?" I tossed them a smile. "I'm thirsty."

Rake consulted with his nemesis. "One drink each," he concluded.

"It's only civilized."

"It's only civilized," Don agreed.

"After all day at the office, I don't know how else one calms the nerves."

"A drink is the best way to calm the nerves," Rake agreed, ordering a Guinness, beheading it with an elongated slurp. "Let's warm up. Let's have a practice round."

I walked with them, drinking quickly, anxious over work, especially what remained. PJ just back from a two-day vacation. Unfinished business at the office. As with sex, there's a point of no return when calm takes hold of the body, but the buildup is all nerves. Even now, Daddy feels it preparing for surgery. Which is why he drinks wine with lunch.

I dragged over a stool and watched them throw darts at the board with staggering inaccuracy. They weren't even playing yet, and already they were calling each other pansies and discussing whose momma would more likely have worn combat boots. Fortunately the place was filling up, submerging their voices in the warm hum of conversation.

To be sporting, Don asked me whether I'd like to play a round. Had they not still been practicing, this would have been out of the question. Against regulations and so forth. Don handed me his darts.

"Best of three," Rake said. The darts were not in good shape, dulled and dented from all the times they'd hit objects less forgiving than the board. "It won't make any difference," Rake smirked, showing me his own set. "Ladies first. Go ahead and throw."

Because I've never been much good at acting like a girl, at losing and being lame and all that, my darts landed where they belonged. Rake's did not, smacking into the wall, falling like birds against a windowpane. Results were similar in the second and third rounds, and the more I punctured the board, the more the world seemed as it ought: completely within my power. The laws of physics are addictive, and more potent still when mixed with competition.

"Fucking unbelievable," Rake kept saying, shaking his

head. "Gotta fucking concentrate. Gotta fucking . . ." And then nothing.

I tossed one of my darts at him. It landed deep in his leather shoe.

"What the *fuck*! What'd you do that for, Gloria?"

"It was your turn. You were wasting time."

Don helped him with the laces. Underneath, his sock was a red blur. "I think I need to go to the hospital. Rabies . . . lockjaw . . . internal bleeding . . ." Already others in the room were gathering to see what had happened. A tourist's camera flashed. "You didn't mean to do that, right? It was unintentional."

"What a silly question, Rake." Nothing I do is unintentional. Nothing.

SIX

MADISON WANTS TO KNOW WHETHER editorial meetings are always this way, because if they are, she has a suggestion.

"Which is . . ."

"Let me run them. I'm good at resolving conflicts and I know my priorities."

"The next item of business will be our cover story. Madison will be exempted from this discussion as she clearly still doesn't understand how this magazine works."

"You're just jealous of me." She smiles.

I smile back. "Use your gift certificate, Madison." I touch two fingers to my nose and make a snipping motion. "With the miracles of modern surgery, there's no reason your nose has to be as big as your mouth. Now, back to business."

"Speaking of business . . ." It's Dan this time. Instead of the usual watch cap, he's wearing a beret, brown and stuffed with his hair like a potato sack. "Weren't you going to bring us sales figures?"

"I don't see what good they'd do. You've seen sales drop for the past three months and it hasn't made your story ideas any better."

"But, specific numbers?"

"There are seven of you now. If I fire you, there will be six."

"That's not what I mean."

"You don't need to know the details. I'm telling you what's important: Readers don't care about *Portfolio* anymore"—I leaf through an issue—"and there's no reason why they should."

"To be more accurate," Madison interjects, "seventy-eight percent of past subscribers say they'd not read *Portfolio* if it were the only magazine in their doctor's office. And one percent say they'd switch doctors."

"What don't they like?" Moira asks. As if it's not obvious.

"Music. Film. Fashion. Clubs. The whole fucking book." I toss one copy across the table and then another. "I'm under a lot of pressure. I don't have time for this." Bruce collects the magazines from the floor. I drink some water and swallow the ice cubes. "I have bigger things to worry about."

"Like your own career?" Dan says, before I can cut him off. "You're never in the office, Gloria. We do everything for you and we can't find you when you're needed. You've even found somebody to put in jail time on your behalf."

"It's not that simple." Emmett says Perry's reached his half-life as a suspect. Brody is going to subpoena PJ's calling-card records.

"You don't *do* anything, Gloria. How do you expect issues to be coherent? Under PJ, this was a great magazine."

"According to the latest figures, eighty-three percent of current subscribers rated this a great magazine under PJ." Madison, again. "Whereas only thirty-seven percent rate it a great magazine now."

I glare at her, but address my comments to Dan. "You're trying to blame this on the Bulk Mail Butcher? Please, Dan. Even you can't pin your own incompetence on poor Perry Nash."

"Five percent of homeowners with household incomes of over $125,000 say Perry would make a better editor of *Portfolio* than—"

"Don't you ever ask anything useful in your polls, Madison?"

"All information is useful if you're receptive to it."

"Then why don't you study the *Encyclopaedia Britannica* instead of bothering our readers?"

"Your *Britannica* isn't up to date." She smiles at me, as if now her numbers make sense, and the lack of a current encyclopedia is the root of our problem . . . according to 12.3 percent of people who have never read *Portfolio* because they're blind.

"How about something useful? Why don't you tell us, Madison, what John Q. Public *would* like to see in my magazine."

"Eighty-seven percent of people under the age of forty would like to see more sports coverage."

"We don't cover sports, Madison."

"Which is precisely your problem."

"And what percentage would like to see . . . naked women on the cover of each issue?"

"Seventy-eight percent of males under the age of sixty, twenty-three percent of females."

"You asked that question?"

"I'm thorough." Madison looks so smug I want to slap her.

"But utterly useless, Madison. You're wasting the time of

our potential subscribers and you're wasting my time. I hired you to—"

"What Madison said about sports was pretty interesting." Moira again, probably vocalizing only to prove she's not fallen asleep.

"We are not *Sports Illustrated.*"

"Six out of ten want to read exposés on sports salaries and contract negotiations . . ."

"We are not *Business Week.*"

"Eight out of ten would buy an issue guest-edited by Dennis Rodman."

"Thank you, Madison." I stand. "This meeting is—"

"Nine out of ten would subscribe to a magazine edited by O.J. Simpson."

"This meeting is adjourned." I gather my papers and I hold them to my body. I turn away from the table and my editors all in disarray over Madison as if she could help them and maybe even save them from me. My palm touches the aluminum doorknob.

"And the cover?" asks Katherine.

"Let's not worry about that." I don't even turn around. "Just do what you're told. If I need your opinion, I'll ask for it."

"Because placing an athlete—"

"Athletics is vulgar. The only reason people play football is because they lack the IQ to do anything meaningful with their lives. We will not have sports on the cover or in the magazine. Ever. Clear?"

"With all due respect, Gloria," Dan says, cranky now, "I think Dmitri should be involved in these decisions."

"You stay away from Dmitri." My hand falls from the doorknob, warm now. "He's a very busy man."

"I'm sure he could find half an hour. If the future of the magazine is at stake."

I wait for him to finish and then I wait some more and when the whole room is quiet and even Rake and Don Richard have stopped playing with each other, I walk up to Dan, just one foot away, and I ask him when he was last tested for HIV.

He looks around. He looks at everyone else and he sees that everyone is looking at him.

"It's not a trick question."

Madison giggles. Nervously.

"What's your stunt this time, Gloria?" He keeps looking at me and then at Madison and Rake and Katherine. "Now that you're getting away with . . . murder, what's your new game?"

"For those of you who haven't heard, Randy will be taking a leave of absence of indeterminate length, beginning tomorrow." I drop my papers on the conference table. "Any names of potential replacements should be proposed in writing to Bruce. Next week will be very busy, for those of you who are still with us."

"What do you mean, of *indeterminate* length? What have you done to her?"

"She's HIV-positive, Dan. She's going to get AIDS and then die. Now quit the chivalry. Please have yourself tested right away and do not fuck any more interns until you have done so and provided Bruce with the appropriate paperwork."

They're all watching me, everyone except Dan, who's now studying his hands and stuttering the same sound patterns again and again. I apply new lipstick because my face knows instinctively not to move when it's being made up. At last Rake speaks. He wants to know when it all happened.

"Does it matter? The point is it's done and now we need a replacement."

"Um."

"Look. Anybody who had sexual contact with Randy is to be tested before sleeping with anyone else here. Anyone who had sexual contact with anyone who had sexual contact with her needs to do the same. I cannot have this magazine undermined by what you do outside this office." I pull my hair back and then let it drop over my ears. "God knows, you undermine it enough by what you do while you're here."

SEVEN

RAIN SPATTERS OFF THE PAVEMENT and wets my stockings as I pace the sidewalk in front of the San Francisco Museum of Modern Art. It's 12:45. I've been waiting fifteen minutes.

"Fancy meeting you here."

First there's the grin, toothy and crinkled at the edges. Then I see it's Perry, dressed head-to-toe in a shiny yellow slicker.

"You're late."

Perry stuffs his wet body into my segment of the revolving door and breathes excuses into my ear while I push our way through. He was being followed. He took an indirect route. He lost his way.

"I think I ditched them."

"Don't be an idiot." In the atrium, I wave to an FBI agent I recognize from an early interrogation, but it's lost on Perry, whose glasses have steamed over.

"Over here," I tell him.

"Will you wipe for me?" Perry hands me his glasses. "I'm all rubber." He points to his slicker and shrugs.

Apparently nobody's told Perry what a dreary suspect he makes. Nobody's explained to him that suspects shouldn't wear yellow slickers, and least of all when they're concerned about being easily identified and followed. The truth shall set you free.

"What do you want to see first?"

"Let's walk through the permanent collection."

Perry pays. We pass the information desk and climb the main stairway. Everything is stone at the SFMOMA, cold and sleek and modern as a Krups coffeemaker. My pumps slip easily on the black marble floors. Perry holds me for support.

"This is serious, isn't it?"

"You could say that."

"And it makes no difference that I'm innocent."

"Innocence is a matter of perception." I smile. "Don't you just adore Robert Motherwell?"

We're standing in one of the countless white rooms stacked like boxcars with windows to the history of art. The floors are hardwood and Perry stares at them. Then he looks up to the security camera. Beads of water relay-race down his slicker. He doesn't see the art. He snaps at me when I comment on pigmentation.

"This is my fucking life, Gloria. It's important."

"Art is important, too."

"I *couldn't* have done it."

"You're a doctor." The time we fucked, I bit my lip and he nearly collapsed when he saw the plasma pooling at my lips. Then I tried to kiss him. He lost his erection as if he couldn't take the blood. "Come closer. I want to show you something."

I remove an earring and with it I pierce my fingertip.

"Don't."

I squeeze my palm to make the blood come.

He doesn't look.

He looks and his skin turns translucent and wet and his eyes shut and he can't. He turns his back. I swab my fingertip with a Kleenex.

"Never mind that. I'm innocent and you have to help. It's only fair."

"Only fair?"

In front of us now are several second-string Rothkos. Perry speaks, but everything he says filters through them, and mostly they filter him out. Van Gogh may have dosed himself on paint for the imagined hallucinogenic qualities of turpentine, but with Rothko, it's the viewer who ends up drugged. The colors, as disloyal to the spectrum as the blue and green and hazel of eyes, seeps through the body like Valium, displacing moods by imitating their peculiar contours. Lies overcoming reality. Lies becoming reality. I am agnostic not because science challenges God's credibility, but because lies determine his value.

"I'm not impotent. You know that. And I'm not a murderer. My life is ruined, Gloria. My wife's leaving me. She believes I fit the profile. And the FBI's found out about my little . . . side business. They think I'm at the center of the Ritalin Exchange and the article I wrote was a publicity stunt." I'm still with the Rothkos, but Perry has plunged into the Pollock room. He's nearly shouting. "*And* everybody says I'm the fucking Bulk Mail Butcher. I could go to jail . . . forever. I'm totally wrong for this. Do you know what jail is like for people like me? Do you have any idea?"

"Quite unpleasant, from what Agent Brody tells me. Uncivilized. Of course you'd be worse off than most."

"Worse?"

"No hardened criminal would take you seriously as a murderer. They would have no reason to respect you at all."

"Then why doesn't the FBI leave me alone?" We've reached Warhol by now. The electric chairs. "You're not completely cold. We made love. I must mean something to you."

"Don't be a fucking sentimentalist. We screwed and then you wrote the article. You got what you wanted and so did I. What more did you expect?"

Perry puts his hand on my shoulder.

"I'm innocent. Why won't you tell people that? Don't I have anything you need *now*?"

"You do. But you're hardly in a position to haggle."

Perry paces from Warhol to Lichtenstein and back again.

"I hear that nine out of ten subscribers would rather have me edit *Portfolio* than you."

"We don't need the rabble. That's what PJ never understood."

"So you clarified matters for him with a scalpel and syringe?"

"You're the doctor."

"I'm not impotent, Gloria. Will you please help me?"

"You'll help me, Perry." I kiss him, on the lips. "Do what you're told and you'll help us both."

EIGHT

GEORGIA MCKENZIE IS OF COURSE A whore. One has no choice, really, if one is to survive as a freelance journalist. Loyalty to a single magazine is more deadly than vecuronium bromide.

Georgia writes for *The Algonquin*. She also writes for *Vanity Fair, The Atlantic Monthly, The New York Times Magazine,* and anybody else with a big enough checkbook and sufficiently pleasant perks. That's why she's always invited to *Portfolio* parties. It's why I take her to places like Elba for lunch.

"Has your new agent found you a suitable publisher?" I ask.

"I fired him this morning. He got an offer from a small press, but I'm better than that, Gloria. I've done this for twenty years and I need a real publisher."

Elba is an American bistro with orange walls and deco light fixtures. Like all American bistros with orange walls and deco light fixtures, it's crowded with darkly dressed yuppies on strict diets. Georgia, who may or may not be wearing the same outfit she did to the release party, is conspicuously out of place. She's not bothered. When the tart little waitress appears, she orders a glass of Merlot and the grilled chicken on focaccia with extra mayo. I ask for the house Chardonnay because that's what I was drinking while waiting. Drinking to survive Georgia and to survive our meal together. I order a bowl of squash bisque.

"Forget infant pornography, Georgia. I have a real story for you. Perry Nash is innocent, the FBI suspects it, and I can prove it."

"Then why do you need me?"

"Credibility. Perry's just the beginning. You're the best reporter money can buy. And you need the exposure."

"I'm to write this for . . . *Portfolio?*" She arches her eyebrows and sips at her wine. "Isn't that a bit incestuous?"

"Everything worthwhile is incestuous. I have a responsibility as an editor. A responsibility to the magazine. Perry will cooperate."

The waitress, all makeup and bones, drops Georgia's sandwich at my place. I object and she rolls her eyes and sweeps the plate across the table. She puts my soup down where the sandwich was. She asks me whether I need fresh ground pepper, her voice thick with sarcasm. I tell her I do. She scatters more of it on my outfit than she does on my bisque.

"I just don't understand the significance, Gloria. What's the difference if Perry's innocent? People are innocent all the time."

I try to explain. I ask her to recall that this is the publishing industry. Media, which everyone's lately so obsessed with that whole TV and radio shows are devoted to it. Law enforcement has every reason to handle it right. If they solve it, they'll look heroic; if not, they'll come off as fools. The case is a test. A test of the law enforcement system in America at the close of the twentieth century.

"The truth is, I make a much better suspect. I've a more plausible motive and obviously the means. Everybody says so." From my briefcase I remove a scrapbook, leather-covered, with pages of black construction paper. I open it just past halfway. To the most recent article on me.

Georgia smiles. "Do I sense jealousy?"

"I'm merely trying to be honest." I skim my spoon across the surface of the bisque and taste the soft liquid while she looks over a *Chronicle* exclusive: PJ'S DOC SAYS 'CLAVICLE OK LAST CHECKUP.' "Besides, I sense you could use a Pulitzer now. Pulitzer winners get big publishing deals."

"And *you* could use an issue with massive circulation."

She turns the page in the scrapbook. The "Sounds & Furies" column from *The Algonquin* with a parody of my FBI file. Un-American activities include drinking Fumé Blanc with pizza. I have never ordered Fumé Blanc with my pizza. I drink Gewurztraminer.

Next page, please: An item from the *Examiner,* with the headline "PJ LAST SAW DOC 3 YEARS AGO." Turns out PJ had good reason to be afraid of medicine.

"The article I have in mind isn't a news piece. It's an exposé. I'm offering you unique insight into the American law enforcement system. Plus ten thousand upon completion."

"I can't work for that." She's finished her sandwich and is systematically working her way through the bread and butter. "I'll have to travel to Washington."

"Travel to the moon for all I care. Expense whatever you like. Write me a postcard." I smile at her because we both know the game is through. No more need to worry about living happily ever after and all that.

"There are interviews to consider. I need to be compensated for my time."

"I'm not *The Algonquin*."

"Everyone knows that is your aspiration." She touches my hand with her own, cold and slippery.

"Then this will suit us both: For every copy the magazine sells, you get a nickel. Royalties. Even Art Reingold would never offer that."

"You realize I'll have to say things about you."

"Write what you believe. I won't stop you."

"There's something more you're concealing. You're too intelligent to be a martyr."

"Were I hiding something, an investigative journalist of your caliber would certainly uncover it." I remove a set of file cabinet keys from my purse. The key ring is Tiffany and sterling. I drop them on Georgia's empty bread plate. "Complete access. Even the FBI doesn't have that."

"Tell me your ploy," she says, but already the keys are in her pocket. "You want to get away with murder, don't you?"

"And if I did, do you honestly think I could be stopped?"

"Are you discounting my talent?"

"On the contrary. I'm putting a premium on it. Five cents a copy. The sort of money that makes news in its own right."

"You do know, Gloria, that magazines don't win Pulitzers. Newspapers do."

"Don't be so literal. This is a unique situation. Crime pays, Georgia. You just need to be in a position to collect."

V. DISSECTION OF THE ELBOW

Make a vertical incision through the integument along the middle line, from the outer extremity of the anterior fold of the axilla to about two inches below the elbow joint, where it should be joined by a transverse incision, extending from the inner to the outer side of the forearm.

—GRAY'S ANATOMY

ONE

I WAKE UP AT NINE TO THE BELLIGERENCE of my alarm clock, consider hitting the snooze button, then realize how desperately I need to pee. Drops of hot urine dribble down my thighs as I hurry toward the toilet. When I sit down, nothing comes. I run my hands through my snagged hair, over my puffy eyes. Then all is okay: a valve drops and the urine pours through.

At five past, I wash my face and start the shower and brush my teeth while I wait for the water to warm. My complexion is all over the place, and my eyes show the truth about my dozing patterns: I've always slept exceptionally well, but now I can't recall how to get to that point. Life has filled my mind with senseless plots and counterplots, and sleep is only to be found at the far end of the maze. What I've forgotten are the shortcuts. How to cheat. I step into the shower. I try to escape how moribund I look because that's the only way to escape how paralyzed I feel.

Water runs down my back while I shampoo and lather. I pick some articles to drop from the next issue. As usual, my editors overassigned, but mostly it's that they're trying to slip athletics into the magazine. Nobody's being terribly subtle about it: a baseball-film mock World Series that uses computer technology to play fictional teams against each other. Profiles of legendary sports bars. These are the easy kills. More problematic is the fuck-and-tell by a homeless illegal alien about her serial locker-room affairs with major-league pitchers.

As I dress, I call the office on the cordless. By now it's nearly ten, and even Spivvy has arrived. I always make a point of being the last one in.

Adam is preparing to leave for a midmorning shoot. While I untangle a pair of panty hose, he complains that Don Richard never has his act together, and Bruce isn't any help. I spot a run. I step into a second pair of stockings and nearly slip on the first as I reach for a suitable bra. I toss a couple of skirts onto my unmade bed. "You cannot shoot the fashion behind Don's back."

"My photographers are better. He just hires people to get laid."

"And you don't?"

"I am an artist."

"Then you must be a good at rejection. Besides, you don't have models or clothing. You don't have a *con*cept, for that matter."

"I have friends. I can model. You know I have unusually fine hands."

"The answer is no."

"Let's discuss it when you arrive."

"You'll already be gone."

"I can wait."

"I have an appointment. I may not be in until two."

"You always have appointments. Where are you going? I can meet you there."

"You cannot."

"Where are you going?"

"I have business to conduct."

"What kind of business?"

"The sort of business that saves dying magazines. And ambitious art directors' jobs."

Adam's still talking. I put the phone in my underwear drawer so I can pull a blouse over my head. I pick it up again and Adam wants to know about the cover shoot. He says he'd like to put Lydia Beck on the cover a month early because of the unseasonable weather. He wants to lay her atop a samovar. He wants her to be nude except for a cell phone and her car keys.

"Forget it. Only twenty-four percent of women are into that kind of thing."

"What's *your* idea, then?"

"My idea is for you to shoot what I tell you to, when I tell you to shoot it."

"That's not how it's been in the past."

"We've not sold any magazines in the past. This month will be different. This month you will not recognize your own work."

"My covers are always recognizable. I have a signature look."

"Better take up forgery, then."

"Who are you meeting with this morning?"

"A writer. Writers don't interest you, as I recall. Since words are just so much gray matter on the page."

"It would help if I could give the cover some thought."

"You're a brilliant art director with exquisite hands. I'm sure you'll manage."

"Why's it so secretive? I can't work like this. I quit."

"You can't quit more than once a week, Adam, and you already did on Monday. Nobody quits more than once a week."

"Then why won't people tell me anything? Why does everybody say they don't know more than I do?"

"I guess it's a matter of trust. I can't have rumors." I yawn. "Lies are bad enough."

Makeup cannot be hurried. It is the single most important element of morning preparation, because how it turns out is who you are for the day. Makeup covers a multitude of sins. I sometimes don't recognize myself in the mirror before I put on my foundation and lipstick and mascara.

I select a pair of modest diamond studs, a present from some forgotten boyfriend, and a strand of pearls. I wind my Gruen Curvex, hoping it will work this morning and maybe even into the afternoon. I dab my neck and wrists with Chanel. Ten minutes to eleven. Jacket and coat and shoes. Briefcase and pocketbook.

In the hallway of my apartment building, there's a large beveled glass mirror. I watch myself walk. I look good.

As good as Lydia Beck.

TWO

GEORGIA McKENZIE IS WAITING FOR me when I arrive at the Bottomless Cup. As always, she appears to be on safari, an effect enhanced by the fact that the natives here all wear black and look down when they talk. They move away from me as I cross the densely populated coffee shop. Her table is by the window. She's found two mismatched chairs, bulky obese creatures from another era. Mine is missing an arm. Hers is losing springs through its base.

"Nice place," I comment as I sit down.

"It's one of my favorites. I take all my interviewees here. When they're not in jail." She offers me some chai from her pot. I allow her to fill my cup. "Let's get started, shall we?" She removes some notes from her handbag, then a tape recorder. "As we agreed, everything is on the record. Furthermore, we've already established that Perry Nash is innocent due to his pathological aversion to blood, as tested empirically on him earlier this week . . . Thank you again for setting up that appointment. He's been extraordinarily cooperative, given his legal standing . . . You will be treated as the suspect we both agree you should still be. As the contract stipulates, even if you go to prison, I get paid."

"Perhaps we can work in a jailhouse bonus." I smile, mostly because it shows off the lipstick, the semiannually whitened teeth, the *wholesomeness* of it all. You don't find people like me in prison, face-front and profile in mug shots. Everybody knows that the guilty are a ragged bunch and the innocent have creamy white skin. If criminal behavior derives from self-loathing, as some theorize, or if it causes it, as others prefer, the criminal mind must correspond to a criminal body. Physignonomy nearly had it right. Murderers do share a common appearance. But it's self-imposed, to be found on the surface only, and where the science went wrong is where so much falls apart: by looking too deep. Appearance is just behavior fossilized. The remnants of makeup and maintenance. The visible expression of self-esteem.

"I'm not going to let you off easy, Gloria."

"You shouldn't."

"I'm not at all convinced you're innocent."

"I'm not, either." I look straight at her. "Just tell the truth." Straight into her eyes. "The truth shall set you free."

PORTFOLIO: Why don't we start with your background? When you were growing up, your father taught anatomy at UC San Francisco. Did you ever participate in his classes?

GLORIA: My father thought it important that I have a background in the sciences. He wanted me to be a surgeon, and he felt my school education was entirely inadequate. He provided supplementary work.

PORTFOLIO: Including hands-on dissection?

GLORIA: We'd work together in the evenings. Dissection takes great discipline. It's terribly involved work.

PORTFOLIO: Would you consider yourself a . . . strong woman?

GLORIA: I'm twenty-seven. I'm editor-in-chief of a major magazine.

PORTFOLIO: Do you remember most of what your father taught you?

GLORIA: I don't forget things that are important to me. Human anatomy is useful. You understand people better when you know how they're put together.

PORTFOLIO: And taken apart?

GLORIA: The dead body affords an intimacy impossible among the living: to physically interact with muscles, bones, organs. It's like the difference between a sex-ed class and actually fucking a guy. Of course there are vast physical differences between the living body and the cadaver.

PORTFOLIO: Such as?

GLORIA: Muscle. No amount of practice on cadavers prepares you for the wet heft of flesh.

PORTFOLIO: Then you've also dissected a living body.

GLORIA: It's common knowledge, really, the character of flesh. One of the essential lessons of anatomy.

PORTFOLIO: What about toxicology?

GLORIA: A matter of life and death.

PORTFOLIO: Would you care to elaborate?

GLORIA: I hardly see the point. Anything you could ever want to know about toxicology is available in a medical library. Dreisbach and Robertson's *Handbook of Poisoning* is an excellent general source, especially if it's neuromuscular blocking agents that catch your fancy.

PORTFOLIO: What's your father doing now?

GLORIA: He has a private practice in San Francisco. He's affili-
ated with St. Joseph's. He's considered the best in his field.

PORTFOLIO: Do you interact with him much?

GLORIA: We see each other socially.

PORTFOLIO: What I mean is, do you have access through him?
Access to medical equipment and drugs?

GLORIA: He works in a hospital. The hospital is stocked for virtually any emergency.

PORTFOLIO: But aren't pharmaceuticals locked away? As con-
trolled substances?

GLORIA: You need a combination to get into the storage room.
On my father's floor the combination is 4-6-3. It's easy to
remember because on a telephone pad it spells GOD.

PORTFOLIO: Have you ever used the combination?

GLORIA: Sometimes my father's late when I meet him there.
The fluorescent lights give me a headache. Aspirin helps.

PORTFOLIO: Is your father aware?

GLORIA: He gave me the combination. They all know. The
nurses see me go in all the time.

PORTFOLIO: Let's talk about *Portfolio*. Has your career there
been a success?

GLORIA: I've been fortunate and I've moved up quickly. PJ's
death created an emergency. I was available to meet the
crisis.

PORTFOLIO: Others were more senior than you. You weren't
next in line for the editorship.

GLORIA: Seniority is about retirement and gold wristwatches.

PORTFOLIO: What was your relationship with PJ like?

GLORIA: He taught me a lot. He taught me about priorities.

PORTFOLIO: Did you get along well?

GLORIA: We were close.

PORTFOLIO: Closer than others?

GLORIA: PJ was closest to whoever could be most useful to him.

PORTFOLIO: In what way was he closest?

GLORIA: It depends. In my case, sexually. But that was only the surface of a greater intimacy. A commonality of purpose.

PORTFOLIO: That purpose being?

GLORIA: To succeed.

PORTFOLIO: At all cost?

GLORIA: Nothing costs more than failure. Because nothing is so extravagantly wasteful.

PORTFOLIO: Is success worth more than human life?

GLORIA: That's why we have a military.

PORTFOLIO: On a personal level, though.

GLORIA: I do not manage *Portfolio* on a personal level. Ultimately the magazine belongs to its readers, and my duty is to them. PJ taught me that. Unfortunately he never learned it himself.

PORTFOLIO: And this was sometimes a source of frustration for you?

GLORIA: I worked hard for *Portfolio*.

PORTFOLIO: Did PJ recognize it?

GLORIA: I was always of more value than anyone else. He knew that. Even at the end.

PORTFOLIO: When was the end?

GLORIA: The last night.

PORTFOLIO: You left early with Rake and Don Richard. To play darts.

GLORIA: Afterwards, I returned. I had work to do.

PORTFOLIO: Was anybody else in the office?

GLORIA: PJ's light was on.

PORTFOLIO: In the morning, the light was off.

GLORIA: I doubt it made much difference to him at that point.

PORTFOLIO: Was PJ alive when you returned to the office?

GLORIA: I had no reason to think not.

PORTFOLIO: Did you expect to find PJ there?

GLORIA: He never left before midnight. Part of his micro-managing. I was the only one he trusted. I was free to do as I saw fit.

PORTFOLIO: Were you his heir apparent?

GLORIA: I was his heir. Isn't that what matters?

PORTFOLIO: Were you loyal to PJ?

GLORIA: It was for him that I stayed at *Portfolio* after my internship. It all would have been different if he'd been offered that position at *The Algonquin*. I'd imagine he'd still be alive.

THREE

FOR A WHILE AFTER I LEFT RAKE AND Don Richard and their darts match, I wandered the neighborhood in front of the office, coat pulled together, hair a tangle and covering my eyes, distracted by questions of projectile physics, restaurant rating systems, mortality. I must have looked like any of the million-odd homeless people cluttering the city. Part of the urban environment.

A man in a parka stopped me to offer some change. I mumbled a thank-you without looking him in the face. At first I was insulted, but then I saw he'd handed me quarters, which I needed for laundry. I dropped the money into my change purse and resumed my pacing.

The sixth or seventh time around the block, our after-hours doorman left his post to use the bathroom. He was old and his bladder was, too. Our doorman always took his time in the bathroom. He was of another generation: when he washed his hands, he may even have used soap.

He was probably lathering when I entered the building. I avoided him whenever possible because of the way he smiled. He always seemed unnecessarily suspicious of my relationship with PJ. I climbed the back staircase. The exit on our floor was mere feet from my office and far enough from PJ to avoid distracting him.

I removed my coat. I brushed out my hair, touched up my makeup. There wasn't any sense in looking haggard, even if nobody would know better come morning. I applied more eyeliner. I admired myself. I admired myself in my compact.

I looked successful.

FOUR

RIDING THE STREETS OF SAN FRAN-
cisco with Agent Brody in the driver's seat and
Agent Emmett in the back gives me new appreciation for the perks of a government job. The cherry light on
the roof of their navy sedan, flashing red like they've just hit
the jackpot, clears traffic in even the most stubborn intersec-
tions. The light is magnetically attached to the roof on a case-
by-case basis, and is only there now because I told them how
much it would mean to me to be above the law. "This is my
lunch hour I'm giving up for you. The least you two can do is
humor me with the siren. Let's drive to Coit Tower."

Agent Emmett shrugs. Brody shakes his head, but the
speedometer is the true measure of his enjoyment.

"Tell us what you know about blood."

"Are we talking platelets, hemoglobin . . . You want to
turn left here . . . Sickle-cell anemia?"

"Let's start simple. Do you *enjoy* blood?" The car starts its smooth climb from North Beach.

"That's like asking me whether I like air."

"Some people are afraid of blood, Gloria. The sight of blood causes some people to faint." Agent Brody doesn't look at me. He can't because, with his car flashing red, he always has right-of-way. No traffic lights or stop signs. No built-in pauses.

"You must be referring to people like Perry Nash." Brody looks. "Perry Nash is afraid of blood." Looks and the car veers left, crosses yellow lines, swallows up sidewalk. "I've seen him faint." An alternate-side-of-the-street-parking sign folds under the bumper. "Incidentally, you're driving on the sidewalk."

FBI agents despise being scooped even more than do journalists, and I know few better ways to ruin a line of questioning than to jump to conclusions. When under investigation, honesty is always the best policy because a successful interrogation requires that the suspect be caught in an inconsistency, subterfuge, and while the truth may not always be consistent (e.g., light is both a wave and a particle), it tends to be considerably more so than most lies.

"You *know* about Perry Nash?" Brody utters while he backs the car over the grounded sign, shifts back into traffic, proceeds toward Coit Tower.

"You know, too, so obviously it's no big secret."

"You misled us. You said nothing when we made him a suspect."

"You didn't ask. I can't exactly run this interrogation for you. I've not been deputized. I have a day job." Gradually the white stone of Coit Tower fills my window. And then we're at its base. "Let's drive to Golden Gate Park. Let's chase down some buffalo."

Brody turns the car effortlessly. Used to taking orders. "By the way, how did you find out? About Perry, I mean."

"Medical school records," Emmett grunts from the back-seat. "He was suspected of cheating in one of his labs because he scored well on exams but never showed for class. We tracked down a schoolmate who told us everything."

"Was he cheating?"

"He had to. Physically couldn't do the work."

"And you're doing nothing about it? This is a licensed doctor, certified to prescribe medicine. I thought you were sworn to protect the public from the criminal element. I thought this was more than cops and robbers for—"

"Tell me this, Gloria," Brody interrupts. "If Perry Nash has a pathological aversion to blood, how did you think he was capable of murdering and dissecting PJ Bullock? You know a lot about medicine, Gloria, more than most. Why don't you explain to me by what . . . miracle he was able to overcome his past to perform an act only somebody fond of bloodbaths would be sick enough to fathom in the first place?"

"There's no need to get huffy with me." I shrug. "Shouldn't you be talking to him?"

"I'm trying to understand why you misled us by leaving out what you knew was relevant."

We're throttling through the Haight. Aaardvark's Odd Arc. Red Vic. Austin Books. "Shouldn't you stop those people? Street vending without a license, and you just drive on by like it's the most common thing in the world."

They ignore me. "This is a legitimate question we're posing."

"Legitimate to ask me to do your job for you? This is fucking unbelievable. You want me to justify your investigation of your own suspect."

"You proposed him."

"I didn't realize I was required to investigate his medical school records before passing you the tip. To first check for consistency. I *thought* I was being helpful. I *thought* I was being a good citizen."

"You were being helpful, Gloria." Cyclists scatter as we rush through Golden Gate Park. One falls off her bike onto raw pavement. Another gives us the finger. And still Agent Brody remains calm. "We appreciate all you've done for us. We simply want to know how you found out that Perry Nash has a little problem with blood."

"I cut myself."

"When?"

"A few days ago."

"You were with Perry a few days ago?"

"You know that. You had people there. Perry offered to take me to the SFMOMA. I seldom get there lately, and in any case, I felt sympathetic. He makes such a lousy suspect and everybody says so behind his back."

"You cut yourself." We drive by the buffalo. They don't even look up.

"My finger." I hold it to Brody's nose. "Would you like to enter it into evidence?"

"That's all?"

"There was an exquisite Motherwell. One of his Elegies. I'd never seen it before. You might consider making the trip. Of course Perry doesn't appreciate Motherwell."

We've reached the Great Highway, beachfront property overtaken by underemployed surfers addicted to the tide. To the moon. Lunatics. Two of them salute. Brody accelerates. I switch on the radio. AM. Traffic on the Caldacott Tunnel . . . accident on the Waldo Grade . . . Names as familiar as brands of diapers and as irrelevant. A pileup of syllables lacking reference. A Monday-afternoon scat. I switch to jazz. Giant Steps, but halfway up the staircase Agent Brody snaps off the radio. Quiet and quiet.

"You realize this new information effectively ends our investigation of Perry," Brody remarks at last.

"It simply isn't plausible," Emmett explains.

"So what's the verdict?"

"I'm sorry, Gloria. We simply can't tolerate obstruction of justice. You misdirected us. The FBI doesn't appreciate deception."

"Get real. You've got nothing. First you accuse my father even though a million people saw him that day. Then you go on to Perry . . ."

"We want you to tell us the truth, Gloria. We think you know who committed this murder."

"I can't. Not yet." Four days remain before the issue is published. Before Georgia's story becomes my own. "I need a week. To put one more issue of *Portfolio* to bed. To consider."

"To consider what?" Emmett asks from the backseat, interested.

"There are specifics you'll want to know. Give me this week. And then I'll be ready for you. To confront your questions."

"The FBI doesn't wait for suspects. This investigation will continue."

"Then it will have to do so without me."

"If we wait, can we expect a confession, Gloria?"

"Better yet, the public can expect enlightenment."

"Two days."

"Six."

"Three."

"Five."

"Three."

"No."

"Four?"

"Four."

"Friday?"

"Friday. You should turn right at this corner." With my hand, I touch Brody's arm. "You could use a short vacation. You look ragged. And your suit smells musty."

"Bargaining is strictly against procedure. But we're willing to be fair with you, Gloria."

"Why?"

"Confession can't be easy."

I open the passenger door because I'm in front of my office now and there's nothing more to say. I wave to Rake and Katherine returning from lunch together.

"Confession? No, I guess it wouldn't be," I agree. I hand Brody the magnetic cherry light still swirling its red beam around as if mixing a Slushie. "Confession isn't easy for *any-one*."

FIVE

'M IN MY OFFICE, SITTING ON A STOOL, wearing a white plastic bib that makes me look fat. Hair and makeup products, none of them my own, are scattered across my desk. A man named Paolo is telling me to keep my chin perpendicular to the floor. A couple of minutes ago he took off all my own makeup with a disdainful sigh and a rapid succession of witch-hazel-soaked cotton balls. Why do all men think they know beauty best?

Adam paces back and forth, pausing occasionally to speak to the photographer. He says he wants the lighting from above and not too stark. The photographer, a small man with a Bronx accent and a head almost completely devoid of functional hair, nods whenever Adam speaks, even if it's to somebody else. His movements are tight and exact, as if set to a high shutter speed.

"I cannot believe we're doing this," Adam says to my face, which Paolo holds captive. "Doing this and rushing the magazine through a day early. As if putting fucking Perry Nash on the cover weren't enough. Our audience is interested in lifestyle, Gloria, not in the state of American law enforcement."

"Murder *is* a lifestyle."

◆　◆　◆

Dmitri said no to the story before he even saw it. He threatened to dismiss me if it ran. We were in his office, and in his office he liked to say no.

"What do you mean, *no*?"

"I mean N-O, no. We're not going to run this kind of crap. The murder already embarrasses me so much I can hardly go outdoors. Advertisers ask me when it will end. It's bad for the magazine and I won't have it."

"What's bad for the magazine? PJ's death?"

Dmitri puffed up like a frog. "Don't be playing fucking games with me, Gloria. What I mean are these shits." He lifted the pages of the article, waved them around—in wartime a sign of surrender. "Why do you want to do anything you can to destroy my magazine? I built *Portfolio*. It's my life. I won't have you wrecking it for some game of yours. You're the editor-in-chief, Gloria. Grow up."

"You told me to boost circulation, Dmitri. You said there were no restrictions. You promised. The FBI has gone through suspects like seasonal wardrobe. Even my father was a suspect until they confirmed his alibi. Why should they get all the attention, and other magazines get all the stories? Why not beat them at their own game and win readers all at once?"

"Your idea is stupid. And so I changed my mind."

"Let me explain, since clearly you don't understand: This

article isn't about PJ or *Portfolio* or you and me. It's about the paralysis caused by modern technology. Countless criminals are running free because the FBI can't see past its computer screens, Dmitri. The equipment at their disposal is dazzling, but they've forgotten how to run a basic investigation. They spend half their day playing and the other half trying to impress Congress so as to increase their budget. Cases by the hundreds go unsolved and forgotten. Perry Nash is physically incapable of dismembering PJ, and the FBI knows it, but still they continue to investigate him. They'll come to the same conclusion about him as they did about my father, but they keep on with their busywork. You created *Portfolio* to take on challenging stories like this. Don't back down on me now."

"The answer, Gloria, is no."

◆　◆　◆

My hair crackles when I put my fingers to it. "Don't touch that," Paolo shouts, nearly vaulting my desk to tackle the offending hand. "You'll make a mess." He returns to his stool, wiggling his butt in his tight white jeans until he reaches equilibrium.

"He's right, Gloria," Adam says from somewhere beyond the lights. "We don't want to lose the effect."

Adam is still being a prick about the shoot, although now the issue is: should I be a magazine editor or a sex kitten? "You don't have to pick," says Adam.

"You can be both," agrees the photographer.

"Two is better than one," adds the stylist.

"I'm not interested. This isn't a fashion shoot, Adam. I refuse to wear my shirt open to my fucking navel." Beauty is like affirmative action: because the benefits are undeniable, the stigma is unavoidable, and because the benefits aren't uniform, the stigma is unjust. I dress as I do for protection. In college I considered dying my hair a common shade of brown.

"With your flat chest, nobody will be able to *see* anything," Adam is saying now. "You don't want to look dowdy, do you? Madison says—"

"Madison is not the editor-in-chief of this magazine."

"Not yet." Not yet.

◆　◆　◆

I returned to Dmitri's office a couple of hours after our first fight to tell him I'd decided to run the story against his wishes. "I will save this magazine," I said, my mouth small around my words. "Even if it puts me in the electric chair."

"The hell you will, Gloria. You think because you're some hotshot young editor and because you have your picture in the newspaper as a suspected killer, you can do whatever you want? You can't, Gloria. Don't be foolish." Dmitri stood, then thought better of it. He lit a cigarette. "I'm not supposed to smoke these, the doctor says they give me heart attacks. But you cause me so much stress. I have to wonder whether maybe I made a mistake making you my editor. Maybe I need somebody more mature. Who is this Georgia, anyway? Your new *boy*friend?"

I told him Georgia's a woman and also one of the leading investigative journalists in the country. I told him she writes for *The Algonquin*.

"So now you have girlfriends and boyfriends. You sleep with her and you think you'll get a job at *The Algonquin*. Why do you stick around here if you want to work at another mag-

azine? Why do you do this to me?" Dmitri lit a second cigarette, leaving the first one, half-finished, smoldering in the
ashtray. He ran his free hand over his bald head, closed his eyes,
and shook until he felt he'd made his point.

"I don't want to go to *The Algonquin*. I'm happy here."

"Then you will kill the story."

"If you want to get rid of me, Dmitri, why don't you fucking do it? I need your support, and you turn around and betray
me. I can't handle this. PJ is lucky to be dead."

◆　◆　◆

Adam's become cranky and says I'm not cooperating with
him. We're arguing about how high my skirt should be hiked.
Adam thinks it should be well above my knee. Otherwise, he
says, I'll come off prudish and hard. I, on the other hand, think
I should look more professional. It's the old bitch/slut standoff,
which is to say there's no way for me to win.

"I'm trying to art-direct the shoot, Gloria. That means I'm
the one who makes the decisions. I can't work if the photographer says one thing and hair-and-makeup says another and the
model says a third. Otherwise, why have me here? I need you
to cooperate with me. I need you to let me make the calls."

I point out to Adam that I am the editor-in-chief of *Portfolio*, which is to say that I am his boss.

"That's what's so fucked up about this," Adam whines.
"Why do we have to run an article where you're the focus? Are
you sure Dmitri okayed it before he left for London? It's going
to make the whole magazine look bad." He removes his
sweater-vest. Straightens his hair for the tenth time since the
shoot began. "This is unprofessional. You can't make all the de-

cisions. I don't want Perry Nash on my cover and I don't want you inside the issue. I've worked here longer than you have. It isn't like this is *your* magazine, Gloria."

"A magazine is not a democracy."

Adam paces the room. "Maybe we can hire a model to play your part."

But of course Adam doesn't understand. I am a model. A model posing as me.

SIX

KIDNAPPING IS A SERIOUS CRIME IN the state of California, though I make a lousy hostage and Deirdre and Emily make even worse captors. But Deirdre says this isn't a fucking joke and Emily pulls out a pair of handcuffs from her black leather backpack and they're in my office and we're alone.

"You need help, Gloria."

"You've been ignoring our advice."

"You've been ignoring us."

"Swept away by Perry Nash."

"We keep telling you to be careful."

"We keep saying to hire an attorney."

"But you won't listen."

"You didn't even invite us to the release party."

"Like it or not, you're coming with us."

I shake my head. I say no. A phone call comes through and I ignore it and I tell them that this is a crisis and they're breaking my concentration. I need to finish editing Georgia's article and already we're in blueline.

To begin with, there's the interview with Perry's classmate, the one who helped him cheat his way through med school, that Perry's finally identified to me. It's an interview about an interrogation, the sort of thing you'd expect to find in some self-consciously postmodern novel but that in Georgia's article establishes beyond a reasonable doubt that the FBI knew all about Perry and yet did nothing for at least four working days. Really, Georgia doesn't know how thorough her article is, or how damning, and the interview will be as surprising to her as to Agent Brody or to Dmitri.

We've also scooped the FBI on the infamous telephone calling card by retrieving phone bills from our accounting office while they were busy seeking a subpoena. The results should make good reading, if you're into the sordid, and all of it in Georgia's steady hand: Turns out I called PJ an awful lot, and for well over a year. Especially when he was away from the office. Nightly phone calls, often past midnight. A lover's calls. All culminating in a tangle to the 212 area code a mere week before his murder. The week he interviewed at *The Algonquin*. And then nothing. Not a single phone call in the final week. A deadly quarrel? A switch to direct dialing? One might assume many things. Some things even Georgia can't be expected to uncover. You, dear reader, are the judge. And the jury. After all, without concrete evidence, everything is suspect. Especially the capability of the FBI to carry out a legitimate investigation. Consider the past. Consider how incompetent the FBI has proven at snuffing out political scandal. Can you *imagine* what disastrous results could be expected given something as complicated as my busy life?

◆　◆　◆

"You two are supposed to be at work," I remind Emily and Deirdre. "How did you get past Spivvy? I don't have time to be kidnapped today."

"You don't have time for . . us?" Deirdre's voice wavers.

"This is my career, guys. You know that. I need to sell three hundred thousand magazines in under a month. The law can wait."

"Cuff her," Deirdre orders, and then my wrists are in Emily's hands and behind my back, chained together.

"This is ridiculous." The cold metal slices into my wrists and I can't struggle because I might soil my shirt cuffs. Deirdre and Emily rope my legs to the chair's base. "This is such a fucking cliché."

"Should we gag her?"

"You'll make me smudge. Please don't."

"Whatcha gonna do, dissect us?"

Deirdre throws a dense wool blanket over my head and we're moving. "Just exchanging some faulty furnishings," Emily explains to Spivvy. Then the wheels of my chair click over the steel threshold of the elevator. "Going down." Deirdre giggles.

They take me to Levi Plaza, dumping the chair, the blanket, and the rest in the trunk of Emily's Rabbit. Deirdre cuffs me to her own wrist and it's a tussle to fit in the backseat together without breaking any bones. The struggle is still more involved on the way out because we're in a dim parking garage, and besides, I've no interest in cooperating.

"Fuck, Gloria. You're hurting." The cuff drags across her charm bracelet, shaving off a fourteen-karat house too tiny even for Monopoly people to live in. She crouches to pick it up and

I'm still on the vinyl car seat, my thighs sticky with warm moisture, my arm extended nearly to the oil-slicked pavement. "Help me here."

Emily rescues us by coordinating first the search party for Deirdre's fourteen-karat house and then my extraction from her car: "A little to the right. Forward. Forward. You're good. Left now."

"Shut up already," I hiss, stepping from the car. "And will you please remove these . . . shackles? I'm not in a fucking chain gang."

"Yet."

"Don't you understand that I need to get back? We ship the final signature of the magazine tomorrow at nine A.M. The signature I've not finished editing. That, if I don't finish editing, will be precisely why I need an attorney."

"You need to start thinking beyond the magazine, Gloria."

"You need to think about yourself sometimes."

"I fucking am thinking about myself," I shout. "I *always* think about myself." But they're looking at me funny, the people passing us by, and I see they're all in taste-neutral suits and we're in the massive limestone lobby of Bickle, Fink & Jensen. I bring my voice to a hoarse whisper. "What are we doing here?" Bickle, Fink is legendary for successfully defending more serial murderers and insider traders than any other law firm nationwide. Billable hours begin in the wood-paneled elevator.

"One of my father's classmates." Em rolls her eyes. "He insists she's the best. He had to call her on my behalf. *Your* behalf, Gloria."

"I've no need for the best," I explain in the closest approximation of calmness I can recall from before this entire ordeal began, as Deirdre drags me by the wrist into one of the famous redwood elevators. *Chink!* A rose-gold Deusenberg drops down the shaft. "Why doesn't anybody trust me?"

"Twenty-eighth floor?" Deirdre asks, pressing anyway.

Em is rummaging through her purse. "You have the key to the handcuffs, right?"

Deirdre shakes her head, brown hair brushing boiled wool shoulders. "You do."

They look at each other. They look at me.

"You can keep your hand in my pocket, Glor," Deirdre proposes finally.

"That'll look natural. Where will you put yours, then?"

"In *your* pocket." She looks at my sheer skirt. Wedges her hand beneath the waistband. I smack her arm. She withdraws and the elevator doors fold open and a man steps in as we leave. One of us on each side of him. We carry the man with us, entangling his long legs in the chain connecting our wrists, until we're all in the reception area and the elevator's halfway to the lobby again.

"Excuse me," Deirdre manages, while the man works his way around me. "She's in custody."

Then there's the receptionist, already skeptical about the cuffs and still more so when Em tells him we're here to see Lolita Jones, Esq. "Tell her it's Gloria Greene."

"But you aren't—"

I raise my hand, taking Deirdre's with it. "I'm Gloria Greene."

The receptionist drops his reading glasses, leans across the desk. "You *are* Gloria Greene," he proudly confirms, punching the intercom button.

We're escorted through posthaste, and only once Emily has seated Deirdre and me chair-to-chair, our hands sandwiched in the soft leather crevice between, and seated herself, too, and all three of us are staring at Lolita Jones's elephantine oak desk awaiting her pay-per-view appearance, that the fundamental injustice of my captivity has an opportunity fully to overtake me. It begins as a cramping somewhere in my abdomen. Spreads through my unfed stomach and then my chest. And my limbs, too, joints aflame. Is this what it's like to be guilty? To be wrongly accused? To be stripped of all defense mechanisms?

"I have to go now," I announce.

"Not possible," says Emily. Deirdre makes the keyless handcuffs rattle.

"I do appreciate your concern, but it's doing far more harm than good."

"You don't need to be intimidated. Not by Lolita Jones. We're both here with you."

"I don't give a fuck about Lolita Jones. I—"

"Ah, the truth always emerges." The cigarette baritone begins somewhere down the hallway and ends mere inches from my head. I raise my chin and what I see is an upside-down Edgar Allan Poe, blue-black hair of extravagant length arranged in a bun larger than a round of sourdough, arms crossed over medicine-ball mammaries, breathing laboriously in my face: Lolita Jones, Esq.

"Of course I'd not realized you could hear me," I explain, standing and taking with me Deirdre's right arm.

"Would it have changed your sentiment?" She moves behind her desk, steps exaggerated as in a kabuki performance. She gathers herself into her seat. The kimono details of her dress float down around her. I sit, too, yanking hard at my cuff when Deirdre attempts to take my arm as her own. "Had a mishap with your wrist? Or have you citizen's-arrested this young woman for some act of mayhem you witnessed in our venerable lobby?"

"Actually, I've been kidnapped."

"Kidnapped? Is that so?" She removes a legal pad and felt-tip pen from the folds of her dress.

"And I'd like to press charges. Against my two captors."

"Charges against your two captors? And do your captors have names?"

"Deirdre O'Sullivan and Emily—" Em waves at Lolita Jones. Lolita waves back. "This is not a fucking joke," I remind all involved parties.

". . . not a fucking joke," she repeats, writing it down.

"Look, Ms. Jones—"

"Lolita."

"I simply don't have time for this. I don't need a defense attorney. You're too late. I've already chosen to confess." The felt-tip pen stops. She sets it on the desk.

"I don't follow."

"Two days from now the entire planet will know every imaginable detail of my past and maybe a few unimaginable ones. Whether that establishes my guilt or my innocence is certainly questionable, as is whether it matters in the end. But there are legitimate questions and I intend to answer them. As a public figure, that's my duty. As a citizen, it's my responsibility."

"If I may offer you some lawyerly advice, Gloria? Beyond the fact that I should be enchanted to defend you regardless of formal charges, confession is generally perceived as an admission of guilt. Regardless of the content. There are cases in which it's advisable to throw yourself at the mercy of the court for the sake of leniency, etcetera, but that's a final measure, a scorched-earth policy. Officially speaking, you're not even a serious suspect right now. You've had your trial by media. But even that's in recess at the moment."

"She's right, Glor," Emily says, but she stops when Lolita puts index finger across lips.

"Nobody expects a confession at this point." Lolita continues. "Who would ever believe—"

"Pre*cisely*." I smile.

Silence. And then bellowing, backed by violent breath intakes. If either Emily or Deirdre tries to ask a question, to raise an objection, it goes unnoticed beneath the calamity of Lolita Jones's laugh. She stands. Performs a spiraling dance on softshoed feet that seem no larger than ears. She claps, maybe for herself. "Simply delightful," she manages, and then her words are hurried off by another bellow of laughter.

"The truth shall set you free."

"Truth . . . free . . ." She laughs between words, sets them so far apart that all interactions of meaning are lost. Emily shrugs at Deirdre. Deirdre shrugs at Emily. The appointment is going more smoothly than planned. "It's risky . . . Very risky, Gloria."

"That's its merit."

"That's its merit. What if you fail?"

"The death penalty is rare in this state."

"Would you request . . . lethal injection?" A hiccup of stored laughter.

"Really, the toxicology isn't as efficient as it could be. Do you think I'd be permitted to propose my own pharmacology?"

"An interesting means of extending the appeals process by a good decade. Tell me, what would you propose? Instead?" Her pen is positioned to take my words again. She sits with the pad in her lap.

"Of course I'm a partisan of vecuronium bromide." Deirdre yanks my arm at the cuff.

"Do you know I once carpooled with Mr. PJ Bullock III? Always so tiresomely self-assured. He never struck me as the sort to take death well."

"When I saw him last, he was in a pleasant mood."

"But surely he can't have known. Known what was next."

"He seldom understood the implications of his actions."

Lolita rocks calmly in her desk chair. Eyes closed now. Quiet.

"Aren't you . . ." Emily breaks in. ". . . aren't you going to talk defense with us? Or backup defense or whatever? Because Gloria can't take risks like she's been. Visiting her in prison would just be too demeaning. Talking through a metal grate. With the guards and all those dirty criminals listening to every word. Gloria's the only one we can talk to that it's not just to get stuff or to be ironic. Do you know what it's like? Do you see?" For the first time since college maybe I think she might cry for me and I'm flattered because I know I'll have a nice eulogy.

Eyes still closed, still rocking, Lolita nods her great, bun-topped head.

I stand, dragging Deirdre's body with me. I walk. Deirdre finds her feet and Emily, too, testing a few sobs on us, and I walk and they follow through the hallway, down the elevator, through the glass turnstile, onto pavement. I walk. We're still cuffed together. We say nothing. There is nothing more to say.

SEVEN

PJ WAS PLEASED TO SEE ME IN HIS office that final night. We'd not fucked in over a week, ever since he'd told me what had happened with *The Algonquin*. As one might expect, that made things awkward between us. As if we'd not even spoken since.

"Let's play doctor." I made myself sound drunk. Familiar territory for us. "You're the patient." I peeled on a pair of latex gloves. Switched off the light and the room turned the color of coffee. "Take off your clothes."

PJ dressed like an old man, and he undressed like one too. First there was his blazer, which he carefully hung over the back of a chair. Next came the loafers, neatly tucked beneath, the left one on the left side, the right one on the right. After that, the V-neck, the button-down shirt, the wristwatch, the belt and slacks. He folded each garment with department-store professionalism, piling them on the seat of the chair in the order they came off. Finally he climbed out of his cotton boxers, one leg at a time, stretching the elastic in front so as to pass them over his erection without having to touch it.

I smiled encouragingly. Undressing others is always such an involved proposition. You do learn things: information lost once the body is stripped naked. But all of PJ's information was spent. His body was merely a place-holder. A corpse.

When PJ was naked, he looked at me, blood-stiffened penis quivering before him like a leashed golden retriever. My eyes had adjusted to the light. His skin was no longer elastic enough to conceal the secrets of muscle and bone: *The long head of the Triceps descends between the Teres minor and the Teres major, dividing the triangular space between these two muscles and the humurus into two smaller spaces* . . . I told PJ to lie down.

"Where?"

"The sofa. Lie on your back."

I knelt beside him. With gloved hands I traced the muscles of his legs, arms, neck. I touched until small parties of sperm emerged from his penis to explore the situation—a dollop of primordial ooze dying off before life was even an option.

"Fuck me?" he whispered, a solipsist with his universe reduced to nine inches of wrinkly flesh.

"Soon, PJ." I withdrew my hands. The bulb of semen dripped down the shaft of his penis. Like a tear. "Soon you will be fucked."

EIGHT

THE GREASY LAMB CHOP STICKS TO MY plate and puckers when I try to move it. I poke at my macaroni, admiring the lubricative qualities of margarine.

"You *like* lamb chops, Glor," my mother reminds me. "I cooked them because they're your favorite."

"We don't eat red meat much," Sidney adds. "Even with a heart as big as mine, I have to watch the cholesterol." He pats his chest, missing the point by a good five inches.

"They're very . . . good, Mom."

"How would you know? You haven't even touched yours. Aren't you going to have some dressing on your salad, sweetie?"

I look away from them both. I gaze at the department-store paintings, the framed museum posters from Impressionist exhibits past, the fake bits of Judaica with which they've systematically transformed their turn-of-the-century Victorian dining room into something out of turn-of-the-millennium suburban hell. Because I so clearly don't belong here, Sidney's house is maybe the one place on the planet where nobody would consider finding me. Not precisely a hiding place, since Sidney has always been too selfish to harbor fugitives, but at least a minor break in the narrative. Thursday night. Sidney knows nothing. He does not suspect.

My face reflects back at me in the glass covering Monet's *Water Lilies*. I stick out my tongue when nobody's looking. I poke at my noodles again, sending several onto my plastic place mat and one onto the factory-fresh royal burgundy carpet.

When my parents were married still, it was different. Debra had taste then. Knew better than to be such a slave to practicality. Sidney has an excuse at least, although by no means a justification. Sidney grew up uncomfortable, the perennial weakling in a poor Brooklyn neighborhood. Let him eat cake. My mother, though, has only lawns and swimming pools in her background. With Daddy she thwarted comfort. Now she's a slave to Sidney's weaknesses. I do loathe her.

"Sweetie . . ." She's still holding a jar of Thousand Island for me, expectantly.

"I don't like those creamy dressings. My stomach can't handle them."

I take a bite of plain iceberg lettuce. Sidney gnaws the last bit of gristle from his lambchop and as usual nobody's talking and then he asks me whether I've yet quit *Portfolio*, found an honest career.

"Gloria's been working very hard," my mother reassures nobody in particular. "She doesn't leave the office before midnight, isn't that right, dear? Are you through with that . . . special issue yet?"

My pulse goes quick. I nod.

"Did you bring Sidney a copy? You know how he always enjoys it."

I slide an advance copy from my pocketbook. I pass it to them.

Sidney spits up a bauble of fat.

"Don't I look nice? I got that blouse in exchange for a bunch of the Chanukah presents you gave me." I'm on the cover because I decided Perry was only attractive enough to sell two hundred thousand copies.

"*Guilty As Charged!*"

"No: *Guilty As Charged?* There's a question mark. You have to get the inflection right."

My mother is now standing behind Sidney with her hands on his shoulders. He brushes them off. Turns to her. "This is your daughter, Debra. I hold you completely responsible."

"Aren't you going to look at the article?" I ask. "The pictures inside are even better."

Carefully, Sidney opens the magazine. My mother says she's proud of me for making the cover and Sidney glares and then he looks back at the magazine:

DID GLORIA GREENE GET AWAY WITH MURDER? DID PERRY NASH GET A BUM RAP?

*How, When & Why the FBI Became
the Laughingstock of the Criminal World*

He looks up at me and I smile as I did when Dmitri returned to the office earlier, relaxed and rested from his London trip.

"I wrote the headline." I point at it in case my mother

doesn't know what a headline is. "Everyone says it's very clever."

Between riffs of coughing, Sidney says he wants me out of the house immediately. He wants me to take the issue with me. "It might be evidence," he reasons. "I won't have criminal evidence in my house."

Of course we've been through this before. Sidney's always worried I'll get arrested for something, as if criminality were contagious and mere proximity could lead to trouble. I try to explain to him the principle of inoculation.

"The police are all goyim," he counters, and then hides behind his beard.

But the truth is merely that he's a coward. In college we went through a similar ordeal. An unfortunate death. Unwarranted speculation. And for months Sidney refused even to speak to me on the phone.

"You can never be too careful," his lawyer told him.

"You can never be too careful," my mother concurred.

It was too much for them. But I was only being honest when I told the school newspaper that the girl deserved it. Her name was Marianne DeMilo. I wasn't ever even an official suspect. Sidney couldn't have known more than the rest when I was the only one altogether there in the end.

Marianne was a nuisance, and in that respect resembled PJ. I only brought her on to run the business side of the college magazine because I lacked the time to be both editor-in-chief and publisher myself. She assumed responsibilities without my permission. Questioned me in editorial meetings. Knew things about me. I'd never have been hired at *Portfolio* had I not kept my résumé tidy. Had that no-confidence vote gone through, it all would have been different. Marianne taught me all I needed to know about crisis management. How to handle people like Madison and the rest.

The technique was suggested by her habit of sleeping on her back. I was aware of the drain cleaner because the plumbing in our dorm was no more reliable than a lie-detector test. I wore rubber gloves and old clothes and sneakers with holes in them. I didn't look at all like myself.

None of us locked our doors then. She was asleep beneath thin sheets when I entered her room. Snoring.

The black drain cleaner kissed her face greedily, trickling over the sides, wrapping itself into her thick blonde hair. I watched but she couldn't; when she opened her eyes, there must only have been burning. Her hands scrambled like hermit crabs across her face, and her jaw dropped as if to release a scream. But the liquid quickly filled her mouth, too, charring her skin. There was no bleeding, only the low angry hiss that acid makes when it consumes flesh.

The acid clung to her fingers. She reached into her mouth. I thought I might throw up. It was all very involved.

Investigators love nothing so much as a motive, especially one with sexual undertones, and that's what saved me from questioning. I emptied what remained of the drain cleaner between her flailing legs. Needless to say, Marianne's semester ended abruptly. Needless to say, my life continued as planned.

VI. DISSECTION OF THE SHOULDER

Detach the Pectoralis major by dividing the muscle along its attachment to the clavicle, and by making a vertical incision, through its substance a little external to its line of attachment to the sternum and costal cartilages.

—GRAY'S ANATOMY

ONE

THE LAUNDRY ACROSS THE STREET from my apartment is always crowded on week-ends, a place people go to socialize while sorting socks. The owners pipe Miles Davis through ceiling speakers, and keep the magazine rack well stocked. For all this you pay a premium, twenty-five cents more per load than they charge up the street. Nevertheless, this is the Laundromat people in the neighborhood use. If only because it makes me feel like part of the community, I use it too.

Early afternoon. At this hour it's mostly joggers and Nautilus types doing their laundry. As if by secret agreement, all wear different colors of Spandex and carry water bottles striped in different patterns. I already missed the Starbucks-and-*Chronicle* crowd, career professionals who wear natural fibers and tend to do their laundry in couples. And I'm hours early for the dipsomaniacs in their jeans and Eddie Bauer work shirts and baseball caps concealing stringy unwashed hair.

I've brought my laptop with me, as well as some coffee, and while my clothing runs through the wash cycle, I compose letters to the editors of major newspapers expressing outrage over Georgia's cover story. I use a variety of fonts and grammatical idiosyncrasies and pseudonyms.

> *To The Editor:*
> *In today's* Wall Street Journal, *you argue that, based on her performance relative to that of the FBI, Gloria Greene should be put in charge of her own case. I must take objection to your analysis. What Ms. Greene's* Portfolio *allegedly uncovered wouldn't pass as a plot in a second-rate novel, let alone as explanation for a heinous crime. If anything, the FBI should investigate her for fabricating evidence. Shame on Ms. Greene for capitalizing on this case for a quick circulation boost, and shame on this venerable newspaper for supporting her!*
>
> *Jonathon Keats*
> *San Francisco, CA*

As an editor, I've learned to mimic other people's voices. This is what a good editor does for her writers, mastering their styles to an extent they probably never will. A worthwhile writer's work is always on the verge of catastrophe. That's what makes editing such a dangerous profession.

My laundry is still in the wash cycle. I open the lids of the machines to make sure they're doing a thorough job. I return to my PowerBook, and there I find Perry Nash.

"What a dumb letter. Everybody knows you're the Bulk Mail Butcher. And you misspelled *Jonathan*."

"Thanks for sharing. Now if you'll kindly get lost, I have work to do."

"I was in the neighborhood. I tried your apartment. Then I saw you here. You look gorgeous on the cover. Did you say good-bye to Brody and Emmett before they were recalled? Why are you up so early?"

I attempt to extract my PowerBook from Perry's hands, but his fingers clamp tighter around the plastic case. The pressure turns his nails clam-white.

"I came to thank you. You saved my life, you know. The story even got me a bit of a movie offer. In Lydia Beck's latest."

"You're welcome. Now let me have my computer back." I pinch at individual fingers. I twist them and bend them at ninety-degree angles.

"You did it because you love me, didn't you?"

"I did it because I love *me*."

And then my laundry is ready and for once there isn't more clothing being dried than washed. The dryers line an entire wall of the Laundromat like catacombs. I find two neighboring each other, and feed my clothing into their great yawning mouths. When I was little and didn't care, I used to wear my laundry wet on hot days. My mother made me take it off, of course, thought it was vulgar the way my nipples showed.

I return to my seat. Perry hasn't left. He taps in changes on my keyboard, mouthing words, cocking his head back and forth.

I take the PowerBook by the edges of the screen. I lift it from him and I snap it shut and hug it to my body and then wait for him to raise his eyes to mine.

"I wasn't through," he says.

"You are now."

"I didn't save," he says.

"Good."

Perry stands. "I want to *do* something for you, Gloria." He leans against the dryers and replaces his glasses on his nose. "I want to return the favor."

"Why do you insist what I did was for *you*, Perry? It has nothing to do with you. You're not a part of this." I come closer. The computer hums warmly against my belly. I lower my voice. "Everything I do, I do for myself, Perry. Don't you get that? I thought you might be useful and you were. But now there's nothing left. You were in the wrong place at the wrong time and now you're through." In sex, men seldom grasp the limits of their significance, groping helplessly once their penis is spent. Likewise beyond the bedroom walls. I often have to remind men I know that it's because of me that they matter.

"Can I still write?" Perry looks at my arms, bare and crossed over my PowerBook. "For *Portfolio*, I mean."

I shrug. "Do as you please. Bruce will route your articles to the appropriate department." I smile at him. "You've already done more for me than you'll ever understand." I lean forward and kiss him until his whole mouth is wet with me. "It's been nice doing business with you, Perry. But I have laundry to fold."

TWO

IF THERE IS ONE THING THAT'S TRUE OF all radio commentators, regardless of their politics, affiliation, or geographic location, it is this: They are bald, dumpy, and fashionless. The pretty boys go into TV, where the prestige is plentiful and the makeup is free. Radio, on the other hand, attracts the sort of man who goes to singles nights, or rather who goes to singles nights smelling of onion and garlic and coffee, and who carries evidence of at least two of these three on his shirt.

I am to be interviewed by Chip Flanner, syndicated media commentator and host of *MediaWatch*. He is a pimple of a man, and, like all men who are pimples, he is very self-important. He has a large stain on his Geometry 101 tie, which he has unsuccessfully tried to cover with a tie clip. The clip has the Presidential seal on it. It's the sort of clip every reporter has at least ten of, but only those in radio would consider wearing in public.

"Now, when we go on the air, I'll introduce you and we'll start with some basic questions about the case." As Chip talks, I pace the studio, studying black-framed photos of him with U.S. Presidents and miscellaneous world leaders. The tie he's worn for his interview with me must be one of his favorites. It appears in his pictures with Clinton, Bush, Ford, Nixon, Gorbachev. If the photographs can be trusted, which of course they can't, the stain occurred sometime during the Reagan Administration. "So I want to tell your story first, and use that to get into the broader issues."

"And Georgia?"

"Who's Georgia?"

"She's the one who wrote the story."

"It's not important. *You're* the story, Gloria. Anybody can write. You're the star." The last of these words he mouths as the ON THE AIR light flickers, then glows. We're live.

MEDIAWATCH: So, why did you do it, Gloria? Why risk your career, your reputation, everything, to reveal the shortcomings of the American law enforcement system?

GLORIA GREENE: I had no choice, Chip. After PJ's gruesome murder . . .

MEDIAWATCH: That's P. John Bullock III, former editor-in-chief of *Portfolio*, dismembered and shipped in small boxes across the country?

GLORIA: As the editor of a major magazine, I have certain public responsibilities. I'll admit it was unusual, commissioning an article on a topic so close to my magazine, accusing the FBI of covering up evidence of Perry Nash's innocence, and of course putting myself on the cover. Risky, too. But, as PJ himself taught me, dire circumstances require drastic

220

solutions. What we're talking about here is trust. Trust in our government and in our law enforcement system. I will never betray my public out of deference to the rules of workaday journalism, and I will do whatever is necessary to get a great story.

MEDIAWATCH: Are *you* the Bulk Mail Butcher, Gloria?

GLORIA: I do make a strong suspect, Chip, and that's why the article was important. The FBI had no good reason to give up on me. I gave *Portfolio* full access to my life so it could accomplish what the FBI never even attempted. A *magazine* scooped the nation's leading law enforcement agency on issues ranging from my educational background to my use of PJ's phone card all through our affair, while the FBI was busy fretting over a common clavicle fracture. The results speak for themselves.

MEDIAWATCH: But are you guilty?

GLORIA: Why, if I had anything to hide, would I commission one of the world's leading investigative journalists to crucify me in my own magazine? Why would I purposefully expose meaningful evidence against myself, face the electric chair, undermine my own criticism of the Federal Bureau of Investigation? No *normal* person would do that, Chip. Would you?

MEDIAWATCH: And yet there's always the risk that your candor will be taken as a confession.

GLORIA: But don't you see, Chip, it was a confession. A confession of collective guilt for allowing law enforcement to fall this low. The FBI put me in a position to make a confession on the part of the American public. They've run sting operations for years, but this may well be the first one they've ever set up against themselves.

MEDIAWATCH: Are they still investigating you?

GLORIA: They got stung. Whatever they do at this point will be tainted. Revenge tactics against the one woman in America confident enough in her rightness to tempt a misconceived investigation with her own body, her own life. A publicly discredited organization chasing the person who discredited them *by making a point of hiding nothing*? A guilty plea just seems too unlikely.

MEDIAWATCH: Until this week, many in the media who watched your circulation numbers plummet speculated actively on how much longer you could last at *Portfolio*. And now there's a rumor *Portfolio*'s lined up for a Pulitzer.

GLORIA: You have to remember that a monthly magazine has never won before. It would require extraordinary circumstances.

MEDIAWATCH: Of course these are extraordinary circumstances, Gloria. There's so much support out there for what you've done, from the media and from the public. Tell me, you have frequent contact with the FBI as it pertains to the Bulk Mail Butcher. You've been the liaison between the magazine and law enforcement since the day the body was discovered. How demoralized is the FBI? Do you think the case will finally be solved?

GLORIA: Of course Agents Brody and Emmett were relieved of their duties, and now they won't return my phone calls. I misjudged their talent, but I did like them. I'm sure they'll find employment elsewhere, maybe in a less demanding environment. New agents haven't officially been assigned. For their own sake, I hope they keep a low profile.

MEDIAWATCH: You don't think the perpetrator will be apprehended?

GLORIA: To be frank, Chip, I'd be willing to bet my life that the FBI will never catch PJ's killer. Obviously, I cared deeply about PJ. We were together for so long. But his is only one case of many. The article was about the FBI, about forensic investigation, not about *Portfolio*.

MEDIAWATCH: Almost overnight, *Portfolio* has gone from one of a dozen intelligent general-interest publications to the national focus of attention. People said your magazine was dying and then you sold a record half-million copies. What next, Gloria? What can we expect from *Portfolio* in upcoming issues?

GLORIA: If you want to know that, you'll have to subscribe. One thing I can promise you, though, is that what you've seen is not an isolated phenomenon. The age of newspaper journalism is over. TV, radio, even the Internet can do anything newspapers can, only better. We are entering an era in which the magazine is the single most important print medium, the literature of the coming millennium. Wherever I happen to be, I intend to lead the way.

THREE

DADDY MAKES ME ORDER COGNAC with dessert, though what I really want is port. He says the cognac is more costly. He says we're celebrating, and we are. We're celebrating my success at *Portfolio*. "My Pulitzer Prize–winning princess," Daddy calls me, and more than once I have to remind him that the Pulitzer's just a rumor.

"When the Pulitzer Committee sees those pictures of you, it won't be."

I answer him with my most withering glare.

Daddy helps me to my feet. His hands brush the hem of my skirt, and he whispers he has a surprise for me at home. Then he kisses me on my forehead, my mouth. I'm drunk. We taste each other. In each other we taste ourselves.

"Will Madison be there?" I whisper in his ear.

"She's still at the office, princess. She says it's going to take all night to make sense of the stats you wanted."

"Well, I *do* need those FBI popularity figures . . ."

"She says you're making her chart by congressional district. Are you sure you're being fair?"

"I'm merely taking advantage of Madison's talents, Daddy." I stroke his fingers. Some I put in my mouth. I want all his attention and I know how to get it. "I think maybe I should run for public office."

◆　◆　◆

My father lives in San Anselmo, in a turn-of-the-century Craftsman house with Dirk van Erp lamps and no TV. On the walls are Japanese woodblock prints. The floors are hardwood and bare.

He unlatches the door and leads me in, his hand tight against my hip. He guides me to the living room, to the dark leather couch where a woman is lying, naked except for a red bow around her neck.

"You got her for *me?*" I ask, turning to my father.

"I got her for *us,*" he responds, gathering my hands around his neck.

We haven't done this in a while, and never before in this way, although Daddy has offered many times. When I was in high school, he'd sometimes wake me up late at night to ask whether I'd like to join him and the woman he'd taken home to bed. I'd always say no because I was already such a problem. Women he dated never liked me. They saw me as a threat. They sensed something between Daddy and me, and of course I was the one on whom they placed the blame. But the truth is that we're co-conspirators, secret admirers even around my closest friends. People don't understand. We know that nobody will approve. But the compulsion is there. Daddy means more to me than anybody in the world because he's more like me than anyone alive. It's not the sort of thing others are likely to understand. It's private. And right now I need privacy.

"She's beautiful," I tell my father. Dark-haired and angular, her appearance has nothing in common with mine. "What's her name?"

"What would you like to call her?" he asks, pulling my blouse over my head.

While Daddy pours two tumblers of Macallen twenty-year, I study the girl more closely. She lies very still, moving only her eyes from one of us to the other. They're green like my mother's. Hair dirties part of her face. One hand covers her crotch.

The girl looks on while we drink, envious. Daddy hands her the bottle. The scotch make a gurgling noise in her throat and then there's no more. She lays the bottle on its side. Approaches him on tiptoe and opens his pants and parts the slit at the front of his boxers. She guides his penis through.

I unbutton my skirt while Daddy plays with the girl, and when I'm naked we wrestle like when I was a little girl and it was a Sunday and we were alone. My breasts rub at the stubble of his cheeks. He kisses my neck, his mouth warm and adhesive.

I hold Daddy's body close to mine, clutching limbs, pressing nose against the indentation of his chest. The hair tickles. Daddy strokes my bare back with his fingers.

And then . . . and then the front door rattles. Opens. When did Daddy give Madison her own set of keys?

FOUR

GOLD-PAINTED COMPUTER TERMINALS, dead but in spirit, line one whole wall of Chat, a cyberbar where Digerati is hosting a media reception. Of course Moira knows everybody at the event, if not by name, at least by E-mail address. When I arrive, I spot her leaning against the gilded computer terminals, wearing the colloquial jeans and T-shirt.

I join her briefly, but someone's deep into an anecdote about Vinton Cerf, and it makes me realize how desperately I need a bourbon. I head for the bar. All around me, webmasters court webmistresses with promises of unlimited bandwidth. Five or six teenage multimedia developers quietly code in the corner. I am in a diode-green room with a tumbler of bad bourbon and I have nothing to say to anybody.

I fold myself into a chair near the back and pout.

As usual, I end up in a series of conversations only slightly less vacuous than drinking alone. They're aware of me, this crowd, but it doesn't interest them who I am. I'm at my most attractive when I pout, and that's why men stop at my table. They ask me what I think of the party, and I tell them it sucks. "Do you actually talk like this in real life?"

"What do you mean?" they ask, these men in flannel shirts, faces buried in hair. I am at a masquerade where everybody wears the same mask. I try to explain and then they offer to get me a new drink and vanish with my glass and I'm alone until others take their place. I can tell because the conversation starts over and the drink they bring me is never what I ordered.

"Hello, Gloria," a man unlike the rest cuts in, at last handing me a fresh bourbon rocks. He's short and lumpy and dressed in black and it seems I must recognize him, only the memory is of newsprint quality. "Art Reingold."

"Of course." Art Reingold, publisher of *The Algonquin*, is, even for those as well connected as Brian Edward Reed-Arnold, as reclusive as Thomas Pynchon. The rumor is that most of the *Algonquin* staff believes he's a corporate fabrication. "I'm delighted to meet you, Mr. Reingold."

"Perhaps you'd enjoy a walk. And do call me by my Christian name."

I point out that we're in one of the less-than-gentrified parts of South of Market and it's dark out and I'm wearing heels.

"Nothing will happen," he says. "I'm sure your FBI entourage will protect us from . . . the elements." He points a thick-jointed thumb at a suited man by the door playing an enhanced version of Pac Man on a demo PC.

"It is a nice perk."

"I really must get around to murdering somebody one of these days."

◆   ◆   ◆

We head down Folsom Street, toward Yerba Buena Gardens. The evening is warm. Saturday was the start of spring.

I ask Art what brought him to the Digerati reception at Chat.

"Is that how it's pronounced? I thought it was *chat,* and I couldn't imagine why there were no French cats to entertain us."

"I'd settle for French whores. But you're avoiding my question."

"You live up to your reputation, Gloria. Nobody intimidates you." Behind him a man passes, towing a caravan of shopping carts, singing "We Are the Champions." Art tells me he's here because I am. "Chat is closer to the airport than your office."

"And why are you so eager to meet me? Are you after a Pulitzer?"

"Let's not be vulgar, Gloria." He watches a hooker cross the street, too stocky to be female on the inside. "It's an interesting night life you have here. Would you miss it?"

"Every city has its night life. I'm ambitious. If my surroundings don't work, I change them."

"You know there'd be some irony if you ended up editing *The Algonquin.* PJ was one of the first we looked at."

"Irony. How?"

"I just wouldn't want you to end up dead."

"That won't happen."

"I know, Gloria."

"You're taking a long time to fill that editorship," I comment after a pause. "Four months?"

"It's like with suspects. The right person isn't easily found."

A police car drives by, slows as it passes us. Am I a prostitute? Is Art my trick? They leave us to our business.

"The story about the FBI was impressive. It made me notice you. As did the cover photo. You have chutzpah, Gloria. PJ would never have done that."

"You're right. He wasn't attractive enough."

"And now your publisher is claiming credit for the article? Dmitri? That's his name, no?"

"He's calling me a liar. In public."

"Are you a liar?"

"What Dmitri doesn't realize is that his taking credit for my article is the highest form of flattery."

"Higher than murder?"

"Murder is an act of narcissism."

Art smiles. His facial features are weak, immature. I make him hold his expression until it seems cruel and then I smile back at him, softly, without attachment. Emotion cryogenically held in suspension.

"Shall we head back, then?" he asks. "I have a flight to catch and I don't want to steal you from your . . . friends."

When we reach the reception again, we stand together at the door. Art speaks quietly, folding my hand around an envelope. "It's a round-trip plane ticket," he explains. "You arrive at JFK Wednesday at dinnertime. You return Saturday in the late morning. You don't mind flying by commercial airline?"

"Um."

"Someone will take you from the airport to your hotel. You have family in New York. Make up an emergency. We'll talk more. And of course you'll need to see *The Algonquin*." Art's car arrives. The driver opens his door. "Keep out of trouble, Gloria. Convicted felons are a dime a dozen."

FIVE

THE SINGLE THING I DISLIKE MOST ABOUT travel is that, unless you have a company jet, there is absolutely no barrier between you and the public. People talk to you. There's nothing to prevent it, no Spivvys to screen them out. Silence embarrasses most people. It does not embarrass me. I suspect that's why I'm often accused of being frigid.

It starts off in the taxi to the airport, with a driver whose grandfather was a Polish prince. At least that's what he tells me when I ask that he take me to SFO. I don't know why he thinks this relevant, except that maybe he assumes it gives him the diplomatic immunity he'll need if he ever gets caught driving as he does. To say he's reckless doesn't do justice to his talent. On streets that are empty, he drives between lanes, honking at imaginary pedestrians, stampeding red lights, pointing out the buildings where people give the biggest tips. When there are other cars, early-morning commuters or postcoital castaways, he slows to a crawl, then floors it and runs them off the road.

The whole way, he lectures me on coin collecting. The whole way, he doesn't even recognize me.

At the boarding gate, there are small children. I've never understood why people feel inclined to have offspring or to travel with them. I don't see why they can't be left at home. They're an expense and a nuisance, and they're not likely to remember where they've been when they're old enough for it to matter. It's like people who travel with pets.

I avoid the children and I avoid everyone else, and I board the plane anonymous behind heavy dark sunglasses. I read the paper. I read and frown and I pretend I'm as stern as Daddy.

"Hello, my name is Rupert." An arm extends across my newspaper, sleeve brushing against my breasts. I look up and what I see is someone who can only be a college student. "What's *your* name?"

"Um . . . Gloria, but . . ." We haven't even been told to fasten our seatbelts yet.

"It looks like you're awfully busy there, Gloria. You even forgot to take off your sunglasses. What do you do for a living?" His eyes will not leave my face. It isn't sexual, Rupert's look. That I could handle. What it is, I begin to suspect, is genuine curiosity.

I desire to tell him something boring, maybe that I'm an attorney or a furniture wholesaler like Sidney. But of course I don't know how to be so dull, and to be caught in a lie takes so much more energy than telling the truth. "I do some editing," I tell him, staring at my white stockings.

"Who do you edit for, Gloria? I *heart* editors."

"For . . . for *Portfolio*," I mumble. Still no indication that our seatbelts should be fastened. Three thousand miles to go, and we're on the fucking tarmac.

Rupert's eyebrows rise inexcusably high. (Is he made of plastic? Does he run on Duracells?) "I know who you are. You're *Gloria Greene*. My roommate has your picture in our bathroom at school. Along with Manson and the Ayatollah. My roommate's crazy. Sometimes he says he wants to murder me. You have to promise not to tell him how."

To escape, I hide in the bathroom. I neglect to take my newspaper with me and so I'm stuck reading the loading instructions on the inside of the towel dispenser until I have them memorized. People knock on the door and the plane takes off and once or twice the FASTEN SEATBELT sign flashes, but mostly it's uneventful.

I remove and reapply my makeup. I do so at least six times over the next hour, trying to figure out Art's philosophy of eyeliner. I tamper with the smoke detector, if only because it's a federal crime that carries such a significant fine. I take five or six bars of soap to give Sidney as a Passover present.

I practice writing resignation letters in eyebrow pencil on paper towels. So many nuances are possible and it's unfortunate Dmitri's barely literate.

I start to write an acceptance speech for the Pulitzer, although there's no opportunity to deliver one. There is for the Nobel, though, and so I work at it anyway: *I'd like to thank my father and Dmitri and Deirdre and Emily. And of course PJ, who gave his life so I could be here tonight.* When I'm through, I flush the speech down the toilet. Nobody writes these things themselves. That's what personal assistants are for.

How many personal assistants will I get at *The Algonquin?* This is a good question to ask Art when I see him. Will I have a car and driver, and if so can it be a convertible in the summer? And what about a private airplane?

By lunchtime I've returned to my seat, makeup just as before

I left. The stewardess says we have an option between chicken and lasagna, which is to say no choice at all. I've flown enough to have established certain in-flight dietary laws, and in these circumstances the rules make my decision for me. First and foremost is always to choose a more solid entree (e.g., chicken) over a less solid one (e.g., lasagna). The more solid the entree, the more durable it's likely to be, and the more durable it is, the better it's likely to hold up if wiping the sauce off with a blanket is necessary.

Rupert, of course, has never been taught this, and so he requests the lasagna, loudly inhaling the steam seeping from under its lid when it's placed before him. He's visibly excited. Excited to be lunching with me.

My chicken turns out to be a nasty parody of Cordon Bleu. Rupert, I notice, is staring at my meal.

"I've never ordered the chicken before. I heart lasagna, you see. It's my favorite dish." He stuffs a spoonful of peas and carrots into his mouth, chewing loudly as if to express his appreciation for the fine cooking. It's unbelievable. There's nothing on my tray I can eat, not even the pink-and-yellow dessert cube.

"Mind if I try your chicken?" he asks, raising his eyebrows several octaves and attempting, I would imagine, to look cute. A story for his classmates. Maybe even a column in the college newspaper: I SHARED CORDON BLEU WITH A MURDERESS.

"Take what you like."

When Rupert has removed everything from my tray and even filled out the meal evaluation form, he unfastens his seatbelt and turns to look at me. Winks. "So, Gloria, what can you tell me about neuromuscular blocking agents?"

We are somewhere over Nebraska. I remove a pewter flask from my pocketbook and take a swig, aching with the injustice of it all.

SIX

SOCRATES IS THE SORT OF RESTAU-
rant that only exists in Manhattan. The walls are
cluttered with old street signs, license plates, taxi
doors. From the ceiling, if the menu is to be trusted, hangs the
world's largest collection of antique ice cream parlor fans. This
is my Aunt Rose's favorite restaurant. It's the one closest to her
brownstone.

Aunt Rose is really a great-aunt, at ninety-two the last remaining relative on my mother's side. That's what my mother
reminded me when I told her I was going to New York for a
couple of days. Since the rest are dead, Aunt Rose is now her
favorite. My mother and Sidney call her every night. "You want
to take advantage of these opportunities," Sidney reminded
me. "Your aunt won't live forever, you know. Maybe you want
to take her grocery shopping as well."

The waiters at Socrates are all intimate with Aunt Rose. "Do
you come here often?" I ask into the hearing aid closest to me.

"I can't hear you, dear. You'll have to speak up."

"Do you usually smell of talcum powder and urine?"

"You never come to see me anymore. What could be keeping you so busy? Are you married yet?"

"I'm about to win the Pulitzer Prize."

"I want to order. Do you know what you're eating?" Aunt Rose calls over a waiter and asks for a bowl of French onion soup with extra cheese, a cheeseburger deluxe with chili on it, and a frozen hot chocolate. Her appetite, according to my mother, who keeps track of such things, is legendary.

"And how about your daughter?" smirks the waiter.

"You'll have to ask her, Charlie. Gloria here never tells me anything."

I order the turkey club with the condiments on the side and a glass of the house Chardonnay.

"You don't get that here, dear. If you'd told me you wanted a sandwich, we could have gone to a proper deli. No offense, Charlie, but your sandwiches are no good." Aunt Rose's eyes sweep the menu one more time. "She'll have what I'm having."

◆   ◆   ◆

New York City is about food, and there's no such thing as a light meal. After the airport and the hotel, I was driven to Art Reingold's flat for dinner. His chef served roast beef with new potatoes and asparagus. I ate more than usual, perhaps because I'd given Rupert my lunch, but more likely because I enjoyed Art's company enough to forget my manners. Mostly we found ourselves in agreement about magazines and editing and everything that counts. He reminded me of my father.

He decanted a bottle of '26 Sandeman's with dessert. We drank and talked and drank some more. While he showed me some of the porcelain miniatures he'd just acquired at auction, I asked him whether I was hired. He smiled at me. He asked me which miniatures I thought he should donate to the Met.

Then there was lunch the next day with the editors of *The Algonquin*, deli delivered to the office in awesome boxes and tubs. Sandwiches of every sort and salads, too. I had pastrami with pasta salad on the side, and a can of cream soda through a straw. One of the editors told me stories of famous writers he'd been the first to reject.

◆ ◆ ◆

"It's about time, Charlie," Aunt Rose says when the soup arrives, the wrinkles in her face as crisp as creased paper. "Where's my frozen hot chocolate? You didn't forget it, did you?"

"Coming right up." While the waiter returns to the kitchen for our beverages, Aunt Rose gets down to business. She never talks while she eats, nor does she listen to those who do. I spend the meal telling her all the most intimate details of my love life. For effect, I embellish: "You have to understand that Daddy's just using Madison as a professional façade. I'm the only one he finds beautiful. You really have to feel sorry for her."

"Charlie, the soup isn't hot enough. Gloria's isn't either. You'll have to take them back and replace them with proper bowls."

"And Agent Emmett, I feel bad for him, too. I think all he ever wanted was to marry me. He and Brody both. That's the real reason they kept investigating for so long. You'd think they'd invent a more original excuse to follow me around."

Aunt Rose starts on her frozen hot chocolate. There's whipped cream and shaved chocolate on top, and five straws sticking out. Aunt Rose uses all of hers at once, accumulating enough air in the gaps between them to make slurping noises even louder than my talking. She sounds like an airplane.

◆ ◆ ◆

That night, I had dinner with Robby Wolfe, the white-haired managing editor of *The Algonquin*, and a few of the more famous writers, Jack Upton, Ernie McJay, Janice Falcon. We ate on the Upper West Side at Fraternité, a stuffy French place where the lightest thing on the menu was duck. As always in these situations, I found myself appreciating Emily's talent for vomiting between meals.

I called the office from the restaurant. Dmitri was still there because of the time difference, and at first he didn't recognize my voice. He said he was very busy. He said everyone else was busy, too. I said, "Okay." I hung up and then I felt ill. I decided it must be a toothache, although that seemed a bit literary, even for a life like mine.

Back at the table, Ernie insisted that expensive Armagnac was the only known cure. Then we all had toothaches and it was well past midnight when the waiters took away our table linen.

◆ ◆ ◆

Aunt Rose has consumed her entire meal. To my horror, I discover that I've finished nearly half of my frozen hot chocolate. Luckily I haven't touched anything else, my chili burger, my soup, my fries, my pickle, lettuce and onion. Aunt Rose calls over the waiter and tells him to put the whole congealing mess into a doggie bag.

"You don't eat," she says to me.

I shrug.

"Leave the dieting to the goyim. It's unhealthy at your age. You'll stop menstruating properly."

"I'm very good at menstruating, Aunt Rose. We need to take you home now."

"I want dessert."

"You already ate a frozen hot chocolate. I have to go. I have appointments."

"*Charlie,*" she calls out. "*Two banana splits, pronto. Hot fudge sauce and butterscotch as well.* You don't find good service in New York anymore."

"I can't do this, Aunt Rose."

"You know you never tell me anything, dear. Have you started thinking seriously about getting married yet? Are you still employed? Why don't you ever visit me?"

The banana splits arrive, large, phallic contrivances that could take a month to eat and another six to justify. With a serving spoon she concealed from the busboy, Aunt Rose excavates.

To prevent myself from eating anything more, and ruining my afternoon and my life, I start to talk. To answer her questions. To tell why I'm here, out of boredom maybe, but also because it amuses me.

I improvise.

I invent.

I tell Aunt Rose a story, and it begins with PJ's end.

SEVEN

PJ DIDN'T TOLERATE FAILURE. SOME-
times you have to protect people from hypocrisy
in ways they might otherwise not choose. PJ's reputation depended on a hasty exit, and certainly *Portfolio*'s did.
A man rejected by *The Algonquin* as editor-in-chief? It implied
things about *Portfolio* that simply couldn't be allowed to become true. The immortalization of PJ was the resurrection of
Portfolio. Sometimes death is the greatest affirmation of life.
Murder a form of respect.

PJ never struggled against the syringe. "Be a good patient," I whispered in his ear. "It will all be over soon." A smile
quivered across his lips as the needle penetrated his bare skin.

I pressed the plunger, gently at first because it's safer that
way. The clear liquid surged into PJ's jugular. His erection
withered. His smile sagged. And even before the onset of circulatory collapse or suffocation, there was his loss to mourn.

While I waited for PJ to die, I gathered up supplies. The

used syringe I capped and dropped into a plastic bag to incinerate once everything was through. This is how I'd handle all the possible evidence: the vials of Norcuron, the surgical gloves, the scalpel, the blood. A shame I couldn't do the same with PJ. Being an editor and obsessively neat, he'd always favored cremation.

The FBI tends to blow things out of proportion. Hair is evidence. Hair and clothing fiber and probably even bellybutton lint. I'd showered carefully in the morning. In the shower I'd shaved my legs and my armpits. In the shower I'd shaved my pubic hair.

This was PJ's fantasy. I am not coldblooded.

In my own office, I removed my gloves to undress. Evidence goes both ways, and it's as bad to find the victim's blood on you as it is to find your blood on the victim. Bloodstains. Dry cleaners can testify in court.

My office was cold without my jacket or shirt or bra. My nipples grew as hard as erasers. I persisted. I unzipped my skirt. I peeled my stockings from my legs, watching the skin pucker where hair should have been. Goose bumps. I'd always gotten them more than others. In grade school they made fun of me. They called me Aunt Rhodie.

I'd brought a couple of extra plastic bags from home, and to avoid tracking blood between offices, I wrapped these around my penny loafers before slipping them back on. I clipped my hair in an antique tortoiseshell barrette, then covered my head with a plastic cap. I stretched my gloves over my hands. My reflection fell against the window. This could have been a movie. A movie with Lydia Beck.

In PJ's office, I unwrapped a tarp. Extended it from one side of the room to the other. It reached halfway to his desk.

When I walked, the tarp crackled like bad reception, and when I knelt, my skin touched static. I took PJ's wrist into my palms. I touched my thumb to his ulnar artery. Nothing and nothing. I put my ear to his chest. No rhythm remained.

Emotions were out of the question. Tears are evidence, too.

In the storage closet, I found boxes, which I stacked at PJ's side. Boxes and packing tape and Styrofoam and plastic garbage bags from the janitorial closet. PJ's new home. He never was one to waste time decorating.

Of course Myra from marketing made the whole plan possible, Myra and her mailing labels. She buys lists, buys and trades endlessly as if on Wall Street, and keeps the labels stacked in bricks around her office. It was with a list of *Algonquin* subscribers that I returned to PJ.

For bulk mail purposes, labels are sorted by Zip, which would have been fine for most people. PJ seemed too worldly to ship to only one city, though. I picked labels at random, pasting one per box. No two limbs would share the same airplane.

Which would help me, too. Since *Portfolio* ships large boxes book rate, it could take weeks for body parts to reach their recipients, to jigsaw an identity, and by then there'd be no doubt in Dmitri's mind who should be PJ's replacement: Me.

But of course abdomens are too heavy to ship U.S. mail, and so the mailroom had to use UPS instead, and limbs were dropping in three days' time. Akron, Ohio. Plainfield, New Jersey. Carson City, Nevada. I alone remained calm in the ensuing panic. People opening festering boxes and calling the local police. UPS offices roped off and searched. Calls to the FBI. Local investigators sent home so the real work could begin. I could see what was happening and I told Dmitri how to handle it. My strategy changed to meet U.S. postal regulations and the immaturity of recipients otherwise urbane enough to read *The Algonquin*. I'm a natural leader. My promotion was as inevitable as PJ's death itself.

I returned the remaining thousand-odd labels. I switched on the light in PJ's office. His wrist made no murmur. I pulled open an eyelid, held his head to the brightness. His pupil was as large as a nailhead. He was dead. The eyes are always the last to go.

In dissection, the first cut is the most crucial because it determines everything to follow. Hesitation is dangerous; a timid hand cannot make a clean incision.

I touched my scalpel to PJ's left ankle. With pressure it found entry. The white steel sank until the ruptured skin enveloped it, reddening where the knife had been. This is not how an academic dissection is done. Dismemberment doesn't interest academics, if only because scholars despise practicality. But muscle is muscle and bones are bones and it's all the same in the end.

It was tidier than in the movies. The blood trickled, like sap from an injured tree, following the path of my scalpel around PJ's ankle. Gently it peeked through the detached flaps of skin. As if out of curiosity.

A transformation took place. Religion generally rejects the body as representative of the person, and understandably so. PJ was gone already, his life cropped perfectly to embody success without downfall. The blood and guts were merely waste products, as all those extra years would have been, to be disposed of in the most efficient way I knew how. Clothes were a waste product too, mopping rags, and as the blood started to clot, they stiffened, scabbed. Blood crusted on his white shirt like embroidery. In the light, odd fragments of muscle sparkled like jewels.

The scalpel followed my will. PJ's flesh was new, as generous as prime rib beneath my blade. His was a body, not a cadaver. Formaldehyde tortures the corpse. The cadaver responds to the scalpel with gamy resistance or flaccid resignation. Flesh urges the scalpel. There is no end to what may be cut.

PJ's feet and hands were easily removed, a mere matter of slipping metal between bone. With his knees there was cartilage, as clean and slow as wax against my blade. I popped the joints across my own blood-stained body and twisted until only ligament remained.

I lost track of my hands as I burrowed through fat and muscle toward PJ's pelvis. I cut until with my thumb I could feel the smooth, round surfaces where bones meet. I drew them apart, circumnavigating the thigh with my scalpel, gripping the ruptured flesh at the kneecap for support.

Then I went for the jugular: a messy thing large enough to hold a teacupful of plasma. I used the back of PJ's blazer to keep the blood from pooling. Beyond that, there was the pop of the blade entering the trachea, a mute space with nothing to grip, and the strain of neck muscle, wetly layered like old sediment. The blade had lost its edge. I was cutting and tearing and all pretense of form was lost. PJ was in a state. He would have been mortified.

Detached from his body, PJ's head weighed at least eight pounds. Through my gloves, I could feel the stiffness of the gel he liked to comb through his hair. I rolled his head into a plastic bag and tied it shut. On the bag was a message warning against the dangers of suffocation.

Once PJ's body parts and his clothing were double-bagged

and aligned against the wall, and the tarp neatly folded away, I stretched a clean pair of gloves over the bloody ones I was wearing. (Would Lady Macbeth have fared better in the age of latex?) I packed each box with Styrofoam to prevent rattling or breakage. I was as neat and systematic as any good editor must be. I fit one body part per box and I sealed them thoroughly, as per postal regulations. They looked like presents; they could just as well have held jewelry or household appliances or any of a dozen things more desirable than a severed hand.

I stacked the boxes in the mailroom. They blended with others already there, off to distributors and the rest. I made multiple trips and when I was through I was sweating, wet wherever skin touched skin. Death is hard work.

And then I was alone and even more so because PJ remained so close still. For company, I went to the women's room, stood before the mirror. PJ's blood came off my naked body with a bit of warm water and liquid soap. I unclasped my hair. I stepped out of my shoes. I stood on the cold tile floor and took comfort in my beauty.

The sensible thing to do was to get dressed. In my office I did so quickly, without looking except to make sure that nothing wrinkled or fell wrong. I dressed and straightened my hair and in the bathroom again I washed my hands of the sweaty condom smell that comes from too much time in latex. I applied more lipstick to accentuate my facial expressions come morning.

I shut things down for PJ. I turned off his computer. I stuffed his briefcase in the back of his closet, beneath piles of old magazines and a wind-chapped bag of golf clubs, a surrogate burial singularly appropriate to his legacy. I arranged the chairs as he liked them and put his desk in order. When everything looked as it should, I shut off his light. This is what editors mean when they speak of closure.

After that it was midnight. There were articles to edit, always articles and reviews and unsolicited submissions generally ill-advised and ill-conceived. There was so much to do and so much more to plan. I sat down at my desk. I started reworking the editorial calendar.

I needed to be busy then. To be busy and not with PJ still, crippled by his deterioration and the signs of it so blatantly obvious whenever I saw that vile body. Once gone, PJ was an inspiration because, weightless, he could fit into any problem or solution, the magic *x* of algebra: weightlessness providing balance. Even that night, his gloriously close-cropped life gave way to my own.

In PJ, I'd edited my first biography. The rest of my life I'd devote to my memoir.

◆　◆　◆

I look across the table at Aunt Rose. She's slumped in her seat. Brown sludge drooling from her mouth, running off her fuzzy chin onto her sweater. Aunt Rose is dead.

Or maybe asleep.

VII. DISSECTION OF THE NECK

Cut through the trachea and oesophagus just above the sternum, and draw them upward by dividing the loose areolar tissue connecting the pharynx with the front of the vertebral column.

—GRAY'S ANATOMY

ONE

I STAGGER INTO THE CONFERENCE ROOM
late, in one hand clutching my pocketbook, in the other
a large bottle of pills I made Daddy prescribe to me because my toothache won't disappear no matter how much Armagnac I drink. A seat has been kept at the end of the table
and placed before me are the new runsheets, a notepad, and a
glass of ice water. I take the water and with it six capsules,
twice the recommended daily allowance.

"Are we ready to begin?"

Around me people talk, exchanging industry rumors
and office gossip. Rake makes Katherine laugh. Moira teases
Don Richard, who in turn picks on Madison. She sticks her
tongue out at both of them: long and dark and pointed like a
trowel.

"Are we ready to begin?"

A ripple of silence crosses the room. People sit. I sip my
water and watch.

"I hope there were no major crises while I was away, and I trust Spivvy gave each of you several framed copies of our best-selling cover. Feel free to distribute them as you see fit." People snicker. I ignore them. "First item of business: We need a decision on the May cover."

"Already done," says Madison.

"No it isn't. I've not been here since Wednesday, and I was on the phone all morning."

"We couldn't wait." She shrugs, looking at the others instead of me.

"We got Dmitri's approval."

"He says you're never in the office."

"It was a family emergency. I called from New York."

"He said that didn't matter."

"He said a magazine isn't a democracy."

My gums have begun to throb again, and every tooth burns in its socket. I fumble with my pills, with the childproof cap. The click-click-click of the childproofing mechanism fills the room until Moira takes the bottle and opens it for me.

"It was an obvious choice, Gloria."

"Really the only option."

"But it was *mine* to make." I stuff my mouth with capsules and swallow them with Moira's glass of water. They're right, of course: For months we've been discussing the Lydia Beck cover.

"Lydia agreed to do the cover nude. On a samovar."

"You're not listening to me. It was my decision and I wasn't here to make it."

"The shoot was done Friday."

"The issue went to press this morning."

"It always goes to press on the twelfth."

These details don't interest me. The pain has expanded beyond my mouth, into ears and eyes and stomach and hands. The details are irrelevant. They're for Bruce and the others, not for me. My staff watches Madison for cues as if somehow she could protect them from me. From *me*. Madison, whose title is consultant and whose experience with magazines wouldn't get her into journalism school.

"We can do another fucking shoot." I reach again for the bottle of pills. I need something to clutch. "This has not yet been decided."

"Dmitri signed off on the bluelines."

"Did you have a meeting with him?" I wipe the hair away from my eyes and then wipe the sweat from my hands onto my skirt. "A meeting without *me?*"

"We had to."

"Adam needed a decision."

"Adam works for me," I point out.

"That's why we went to Dmitri."

"He says all decisions need to go through him now."

"He says your covers never move and on his first try he sold every single issue."

"He credits *Madison* with helping him."

"This is unacceptable." I drink all of Moira's water and then I take Don Richard's. I force down two more pills. I stare at Madison and she stares right back. Like the night with Daddy. "Totally fucking unacceptable. This meeting is adjourned."

"We still haven't—"

"Adjourned."

"Dmitri also said—"

"Ad*journed*." I slap the table with the bottle of painkillers, sending the red-and-black capsules spinning like roulette wheels. The others stare at me. They leave and they don't speak. Madison blows me a kiss.

TWO

 PIVVY SAYS DMITRI'S OUT FOR THE day and she can't say where he's gone.

"Can't or won't?"

"Aren't we in a snit this morning?"

"Give me details. I need to know, Spivvy." She says nothing. Spivvy sits at her desk in reception, her flat black sneakers sticking out, and she says nothing at all. She files her nails. "When did he leave?"

"At ten. I guess. I don't know, Gloria. He said he'd be gone for the day. He took Hillary with him."

"Who's Hillary?"

"The new intern. You were away."

I hear clicking and then realize it's my own hands twisting the childproof cap again. Dmitri isn't supposed to be interested in interns. He's supposed to be interested in me.

Spivvy reaches to help with the pills.

"Don't touch me. I haven't got fucking time for twenty

questions, Spivvy. Now tell me where Dmitri and that prostitute went."

She drops her hands to her lap.

"He didn't say, Gloria. I didn't ask."

"What does she look like?"

"Like you. Younger."

"Why didn't you find out what they're doing? How young is she? Is she underage? You're supposed to know these things, Spivvy. You're the fucking receptionist. It's not like your job's challenging."

"*You* never tell me anything, Gloria. You still haven't explained what you've been doing since Wednesday," she says, her voice small and precise. I can't return her stare. I can't look at her. My eyes won't focus on anything, anything at all.

"It was a family emergency. That's all you need to know. I don't have to explain. I'm the editor-in-chief. I don't have to explain anything to you." We stare at each other. "Has someone named Art Reingold called?"

"Reingold? Is he on the FBI detail? They called for you several times during the editorial meeting."

A short man in a bad suit is in the reception area, waiting for his appointment. He wants to leave his name with Spivvy. I tell him we're busy. I say we don't care what his name is and he'll have to come back later. He nods and gathers his papers.

"What did you do that for?"

"He was rude. His suit was polyester. Now will you please help me, Spivvy? I don't have time for this fucking bullshit. Since when are you loyal to Dmitri?"

"I wish I could be of assistance. If he calls, I'll transfer him through to you. And that Reingold gentleman, too. I just don't have an answer, Gloria. Honest injun."

"Well, find one. Or you're fired. You and Hillary and everybody else. I have important business to discuss and I want Dmitri here." I head for his office.

"Where are you going, Gloria?"

"That's fucking irrelevant." I need to examine my contract. I need some Russian vodka. "Tell people I'm in a meeting. Tell them I'm ransacking Dmitri's desk. Tell them they can go fuck themselves for all I care."

THREE

SO NOW SOME WOMAN IS SEATED behind my desk, drinking coffee from a paper cup and staining the wood because she's neglected to bring a coaster. "Excuse me," I interrupt her mid-sip. "You're staining the mahogany. You really mustn't put your cup directly on the desktop. Or, better yet, you could remove yourself from my office before I have the police do it for you."

Her thin lips bend into a smile. We stare at each other. The suit she's wearing is all business, wool and more conservative than the editorial page of *The Wall Street Journal*, but hers is not the overcooked executive physique of early-morning stairmastering doing battle with late-afternoon martini mix-and-match. Were it not for the scar above her right eye, she might even be pretty.

"I thought you didn't trust the law enforcement system," she responds at last, setting down the coffee cup, using my face on *Portfolio*'s cover as her coaster. "Won't you join me on the roof for a moment? There are some matters we need to sort out."

"You heard what happened to the previous detail? To Brody and Emmett?"

"Yes. I was the one who ordered their dismissal."

"Tyra Crimpp. Georgia has such fond memories of her time with you. But you must have made a wrong turn. You're over three thousand miles off the Beltway."

She emerges from my seat. Fully vertical, she reaches well over six feet. "Like you, Ms. Greene, I don't make wrong turns. Shall we?"

I follow. We climb the back staircase, silent except for the stale clop-clop-clop of heels against enclosed wooden steps. I mash the paintless metal door twice, three times, with my body. Wind smacks it against the side of the building. Whistles through the hinges. I crunch onto gravel, grip my skirt with both hands because all my underwear is dirty and I'm wearing only scratchy stockings underneath.

"Satisfied?" I ask, turning back. "Fog looks the same from the roof as it does from the bar across the street."

"Nonsense. Bars are dark and musty. Like prison."

"I wouldn't know." I shrug. "I've not been to prison. I guess I'm not the type."

Tyra Crimpp crosses the gravel to the building's unrailed ledge. She looks down. Kicks a few pebbles free. They scatter on the pavement below. "I would have to agree with you, Ms. Greene. Such a waste of talent."

"You enjoy *Portfolio*."

"That, too, I suppose." She crosses to the steam chimneys, five of them emerging from the roof aligned in height order like organ pipes. She leans against the tallest. "You don't belong in prison, Gloria . . . any more than our agency belongs on the David Letterman show."

"The United Nations isn't one of the top ten places to recruit new FBI agents?"

"The Federal Bureau of Investigation takes itself very seriously. You should take it seriously, too."

"Why, pray tell?"

"How about the top ten reasons, Gloria? How about because (10) the evidence you published against yourself in your legendary cover story, whatever your queer motives may have been, is enough to help us send you to jail without passing go or collecting $200, (9) even if it isn't, it's enough to keep our investigation active indefinitely, (8) we will put so many agents on the case you'll have to wait in line to ride the elevator to work, (7) the agents will find sufficient evidence against you eventually, (6) you will go to prison then, (5) meaning you'll lose your job, (4) meaning it won't make any difference whether *Portfolio* wins a Pulitzer, (3) because Georgia will get back the credit you've stolen from her, (2) you will be forgotten, and (1) prison regulations being prudish and old-fashioned, you will never have sexual intercourse with dear ol' Dad again." She sighs. "Pretty funny, wouldn't you agree?"

"You want something. Tell me."

"What makes you so sure you're in a position to provide it?"

"You're here. Alone."

"With a mind like yours, Gloria, you should join the Bureau." She paces. The wind washes her hair around, stretches her suit tight against her body. "But you'll have to watch your criminal record."

"You obviously don't have enough to arrest me. You want some sort of retraction."

"You, Gloria, are our prize suspect. That won't change."

"Of course I can't help you."

"Still afraid of losing that Pulitzer? Let's not be a pig, dear."

"You don't see." No Pulitzer means no *Algonquin* means no career. Anticlimax. At least there's drama to trial by jury, public sentencing, incarceration, iron and concrete, the electrical surge of midnight. There's honor among thieves. Without closure, what will remain?

"We wouldn't seek the death penalty. Fifty years of prison won't make you a martyr. Just a pathetic old lady." She approaches the doorway. The distance between us makes her shout. Makes her shout into the wind. "We're reasonable people at the Bureau. You help us and we'll help you. Sometimes evidence vanishes. Cancer goes into remission. A hot case becomes another file in another cabinet in another back room deep beneath the FBI building. I'll be reading *Portfolio* fondly in the days to come." She clops down a couple of steps. I approach the door. "Just tell the truth, Gloria. The truth shall set you free."

Clopclop-clop-clop.

The tar paper by the steam chimneys is brushed clear of pebbles. On my knees, I grasp stones from nearby. I scatter them over the bare patches. Wind flaps my skirt freely. Throbbing teeth. Jagged stones. My painkillers are downstairs. In my mouth the stones make my gums bleed. I drink the blood, dirty with tar, but it's not enough. Spit out, the stones are darker. Connected by a web of saliva. Toxic, intoxicating. To drink to numbness or pain or both. I stand. I walk toward my dark and musty prison.

FOUR

AS AN EMERGENCY MEASURE, DEIRDRE and Emily have taken me to lunch at Pinto, one of those Mexican restaurants that somehow forgets to be ethnic. I should have told them nothing when they discovered me, but even I had trouble finding the right lies after Spivvy said I'd gone out drinking at eleven in the morning.

"We're here for you, Gloria," Emily says. "Don't ever feel like you have to drink alone."

"We won't make you go to an attorney again," continues Deirdre. "You and Lolita Jones were right. We were wrong. You can trust us."

"We should order some bowls of guacamole." I'm squinting, still trying to adjust to the bleached whiteness of Pinto after the solitary confinement of Nooner's Tavern.

"Anybody got some coke?"

"What *has* gotten into you, Glor?"

"Death, destruction, and spontaneous combustion." I fill our margarita glasses from the carafe. In mine I drop a handful of aspirin. "I'd like to propose a toast to all my dear friends at *Portfolio*."

"Get over it. You can't expect to be on the cover *every* month. Anyway, I thought you said you were going to win the Pulitzer."

"I probably will. And then I'm going to get out of magazine publishing. There's no future."

Nobody says anything.

"What about you guys? You're in advertising, Em, and you're not exactly a rocket scientist. How tough can it be?" Emily drinks. Chips and salsa arrive, and two large stone bowls of guacamole. Deirdre carefully touches the edge of a chip to the salsa. I plunge three at once deep into the guacamole. "Would I make a good account executive?"

"No."

"Then I'll go into human resources with Deirdre." I refill our margarita glasses and order another round. I also order appetizers, then plates of chicken and pork and fish. "To our deaths!"

"Why don't you tell us what really happened in New York?" Emily asks.

"I already did. I told you everything."

"*Every*thing? Gloria, people who are on the verge of winning a Pulitzer Prize don't dip out of work for a pitcher of bourbon at Nooner's Tavern."

"I'm a fucking adult. It's not like I'm breaking any laws."

"Tell us about New York."

"Like I said, a funeral is a funeral. My Uncle Henry was old. We were close, but I'm over it now."

"I thought you said it was your Uncle Frederick," Deirdre interrupts. She's now eating the cilantro garnish from my plate.

I tell her I don't have an Uncle Frederick and I don't know what she's talking about and it would be nice if she actually listened when I told her things. The best strategy when caught in an inconsistency is to up the ante. If you're willing to call other people liars, they'll never suspect you of being one.

"You never introduced me to your Uncle Henry," Emily says while I drink from her glass.

"He was deaf."

"Oh."

"Let's hear more about Perry Nash," Emily tells Deirdre then, through with the topic. They both know what I think of the arrangement and what I think of Perry in particular. He's seeing Deirdre to keep tabs on me. Deirdre's seeing him to be as I am.

"I love the way his face crinkles when he smiles. He does that for me, although he's still recovering. You caused him an awful lot of stress, Glor."

"I saved him from the electric chair."

"He doesn't think so. Not since he started with his new analyst." Deirdre finishes off the cilantro. She tries one of the tamales and makes a face into her margarita. "How can you eat that, Gloria? Let's get some shrimp."

"What do you mean, he doesn't think I bailed him out?"

"To be blunt, he doesn't like you very much, Gloria. At the least, he says you're responsible for the investigation of his med school records. He may lose his license."

"Cheating is illegal. He should lose it, and besides he's busy making that stupid movie now. Let's talk about something else."

"I want to hear more," Emily cuts in quickly, ever eager to hear smut. "So did you screw him yet?"

"Spare me, please." I finish what remains in the margarita pitcher. When I order another, Deirdre asks for a plate of barbecued shrimp. "What we need to talk about is my career. This is serious."

"*I* want to hear about her date with Perry," Emily insists.

"It is a good story," Deirdre agrees.

"*I* don't. I'm not interested."

"Then leave."

I do. Behind me I hear Deirdre launch into her story. They don't stop me, although I walk slowly enough to give them time. I push at the door. The door is shut. I push at the door and the door pushes back. I lean into it, palms flat against the cold glass. Pounding. Fists. Dented knee. Fractured clavicle.

"*Pull*, Señorita."

When I return to our table, they're still talking, about Perry and about Lydia Beck and the rest. As if I weren't part of everything. As if I weren't the prime mover. Emily pokes her fork at a tamale. Deirdre nibbles some cilantro.

"Hi." I smile at them.

Deirdre tells Emily that she and Perry might get engaged.

FIVE

I DON'T DESPISE YOU, GLORIA," WESLEY
Straus complains, his breath heavy on the phone. Probably a large man. He should go on a diet. "I don't even
know you. I'm just doing this as a favor to *Portfolio*. Because PJ
was a friend."

"With friends like you . . ."

"At least I didn't murder him."

"What's that supposed to mean?" I lean back in my chair.
"I'm the one looking for the killer. I commissioned that cover
story. I risked my career for PJ. And you're telling me it's not
good enough for the Pulitzer? You're saying the Pulitzer in investigative journalism is going . . . unawarded this year?"

"It happens. Besides, Gloria, you knew it was a stretch.
Joseph Pulitzer himself mandated that the award was only for
newspapers."

"You're on the fucking committee. How could you let it
happen? Pressure from the FBI? *Coward*ice." I kick over my

bottle of painkillers with my foot, spilling them across my desk and onto the floor. I reach down and swallow two more. "How could you do this to PJ? Last year the prize went to a story on house paint."

"There was lead in it. Children were dying."

"What do I care if children were dying?" Words stick in my throat like thistles. I'm shivering. "Children die all the time."

"There are years of precedent, Gloria. You know that. Although Pulitzer probably would have approved of your little stunt."

"That was not a stunt. It was serious journalism."

I want to cry but I can't because my eye makeup isn't waterproof and besides nobody's watching. I tear at one of the runs in my stockings and my skin is bumpy with cold. Goose pimples. I cannot escape those. I look at myself, and what I look like is a large pale featherless bird.

"The Pulitzer is not a democracy, Gloria."

"What can you mean?" I've opened the bottle of bourbon I keep in the office for medical emergencies such as this, and I begin to drink my way through it as I speak. "Is this my fucking punishment?"

I dial Art Reingold's office but it's too late and even his voice mail won't pick up. So I call Brian Edward Reed-Arnold. Investment bankers are always at work because money is timeless.

"You have to help me. I need Art's home number."

"Who is this?"

"Gloria. Gloria Greene."

"Oh, hi, Gloria. I haven't heard from you in ages. Staying out of trouble, I hope?"

"Art's home number. Do you have it?"

"I'm doing well. I'm getting married soon. I'm not sure whether you knew that."

"So you don't have Art Reingold's number? You don't have it anywhere in your whole fucking Rolodex?"

"I was just in Athens on business. I thought of you. I though—"

I hang up. I slam down the phone receiver again and again and then I dial my father so he can comfort me. He never asks me if I'm okay anymore. Daddy likes to be proud of me because it's a socially acceptable form of narcissism. My failures assault his self-esteem.

I call Daddy's office and argue with the answering service, more because I need somebody to abuse than because I believe the woman on the line knows anything I don't. I call him at home. The phone rings and someone answers and it's Madison and in the background I can hear my father shouting. "Get back here!" he says. "I'm not through with you yet." I throw the phone at my door. The receiver hits Dmitri in the mouth. I claw at my stockings.

"What was that for?" He sees the half-spent bottle of bourbon on my desk. The bottle of bourbon and the painkillers scattered across the floor like insects. "Are you crying, Gloria?"

I explain that I'm trying not to because of the makeup. I show him my stockings, the loose strands of nylon bunching like dreadlocks. "I keep tearing and I can't stop." I tip the bottle to my mouth until it burns, then drop my head back so it trickles down my throat. "I think I need a cigarette. Let me have one of yours. By the way, we lost the Pulitzer."

Dmitri hands me a pack of Marlboros, crumpled and dusty with pocket lint. I take one to my lips, drop the box by my bottle. "I need a light."

He holds out a match for me, bending forward until his tie meets my desk. I tell him he might as well give me the whole book since I'm taking the rest of his cigarettes and any other packs I find in his desk. He reminds me that I don't smoke. I remind him that I do in circumstances such as this.

"And theses circumstances, what are they?" he asks, balancing on his little feet.

"I just told you, Dmitri. We didn't get the fucking Pulitzer."

"What difference does it make? Lots of people don't get Pulitzers. PJ never got any Pulitzers, I don't think."

"No, he didn't." I inhale on my cigarette, greedy for nicotine, greedy for tar and the hundreds of other carcinogens packed into every stick. "Magazines aren't supposed to win. We could have, though, and we almost did. Do you realize how close we came? How fucking close?"

"There's no need getting worked up, Gloria. Tell me what issue you're talking about."

"Doesn't this make any difference to you, Dmitri? Don't you understand how important it is?" I flick the ash from the end of my cigarette into the cap of the Jim Beam bottle. I've nearly sucked it down to the filter, but can't bear the thought of letting any tobacco go unconsumed. "It was my story, Dmitri. The one with *me* on the cover, that you're telling people was *your* idea, was the one up for the Pulitzer."

"So you're upset because they don't think you're pretty enough? Why do you care about this prize so much? Anybody can win a prize. In high school, I earned many, some for English . . . and for gymnastics. Sometimes I don't understand you, Gloria. You care about things that don't matter except for your ego. You act like *Portfolio* is created by your work alone, and it's not enough that I make you a star."

I stare at Dmitri through slit eyes. He's seated on my couch, cradling his large bald head in his palm, like a basketball. How can he fail to grasp the importance? How can he lie? I face a fate worse than conviction and he doesn't get it.

"This is my career. It has nothing to do with ego. My career is at stake, Dmitri. My fucking *career*."

"Some don't have the same career always. I was trained as a civil engineer."

"Back to threats, are we? How quaint. After I saved your fucking magazine. Have you already discussed this with my staff? With Madison?"

"I already explained to you: Decisions had to be made about the cover, and you weren't in the office to make them. The magazine can't always wait for you, Gloria."

"It was a family emergency."

"Your problems can only take up so much of my time."

"I don't find you in the office much lately." I light another cigarette and toss the burning match at Dmitri. "Spivvy never knows where you are."

"I don't have to justify myself to you, Gloria. I have important business."

"Like banging the new intern before she's been here long enough to appear on the masthead? Spivvy was right. Hillary does look like a younger version of me. Am I too old for you, Dmitri? Is that the problem?" I pull at the buttons of my shirt. I try to stand, and I can't. "You don't like my body so much now that you have her too?"

"Stop it, Gloria. You're drunk."

"Brilliant fucking deduction, Sherlock. I'm drunk *and* I'm just getting started."

"This is serious, what I'm telling you. Your behavior is unacceptable, Gloria."

"Because I told people you're a cheating Stalinist bastard or because all the wire services picked it up? I'm quotable, Dmitri, and besides it's true."

"You refuse to share credit for *Portfolio*'s success. You give others only blame."

"The cover story was *my* idea. *I* commissioned it."

"I have no ego, Gloria. Madison said I should take responsibility. For your sake. For the sake of the magazine. That way nobody questions your motives."

"You consulted with Madison? This is the story you threatened to kill."

"I should have fired you on the spot."

"Except that it sold too well?"

"You're lucky."

"That wasn't luck. It was me."

"What if you'd been wrong?"

"I'm never wrong. I—"

"Let me finish, Gloria. You run a cover story against my wishes. You call me a liar in public. You tell Spivvy you're going to terminate her."

"Are you screwing her too?"

"Stop changing the subject, Gloria. You make me worry. You're dishonest to me and you have no respect for this magazine. I wonder if maybe something really is wrong with you." He squints at me. "Did you ever consider a leave of absence? It would give you time for family emergencies. Or for *The Algonquin*. Maybe you'd be happier."

"It's not that simple. Anymore." I take another cigarette and this time drop the match into the half-empty bourbon bottle. I inhale and I break off the filter and try inhaling again, sucking paper-sharp ribbons of tobacco into my mouth.

"Then I will make it simple for you. Effective immediately, you are on paid vacation."

"I have a magazine to run."

"No, Gloria. *I* have a magazine to run."

"You're barely literate."

"Your paid vacation will last one month, during which time your services will not be needed. Or wanted. At the end of that month, we will decide on future arrangements."

"Are you trying to fucking fire me?"

"You will clear out your office tonight."

"My office?"

"Madison cannot work from an intern cubicle."

"Madison in my office?"

"Madison's office. While you take your paid vacation."

"There are stories I've assigned. A follow-up to our sellout cover. Some facts may have been wrong."

"You get facts wrong and now I'm to trust you to get them right? No, thank you. You are a disease, Gloria. You stay away from this office. We'll meet when your paid vacation is over. Please get the rest you need. I feel sorry for you."

My voice is soft when I speak, softer than I mean it to be and softer than either of us expects. "Will you please leave now? Will you leave me alone?" I hear myself sobbing and then gradually I feel the warm streaking of tears against my sore cheeks. I'm talking to Dmitri, although really it could be anyone: Deirdre and Emily, Daddy, the FBI. The most famous editor on the planet and I can't even run a short retraction in my own magazine. The most famous magazine-editor-turned-convict on the planet.

"It's not healthy for you to smoke tobacco too much without the filter." He hands me an envelope. An open plane ticket to JFK. "You spend time with your family. I care about you, Gloria. You're like a daughter to me."

I ignore him. I focus on the pack of cigarettes, reading the Surgeon General's warning over and over. This pack is only dangerous to pregnant women. I'll have to go out and find one that causes heart disease. I want my autopsy to be interesting. I want multiple causes of death because that's the closest thing to literary ambiguity you can achieve on the autopsy table or in life.

SIX

EVERYBODY AT THE ABSINTHE CLUB'S first anniversary is over sixty, and I've come only at Dmitri's insistence. He calls me daily to make sure I'm getting out of the house. That I'm still alive.

The Absinthe Club is full of fake palm trees with large coconut-shaped lightbulbs. An elderly black man in a white dinner jacket sings Glenn Miller standards to the accompaniment of a graying three-piece swing band. The Absinthe Club simultaneously represents the height of retro chic and the depth of good taste.

Once my coat has been taken, I head to the oak-and-brass bar, which in more aqueous circumstances might be mistaken for the bow of a vintage power boat. I put in a drink request for a gimlet and am handed a martini. I don't complain. Everybody around me is sipping either champagne or martinis, and there's nothing worse than being alone at somebody else's party with the wrong drink.

My martini tastes of cold, and the gin is crisp and quick on the tongue. I am alone at the bar and everyone else at the bar is alone, too. The couples are in line at the buffet or already seated at the small round tables polkadotting the room. The band is playing "Chattanooga Choo-Choo." *You leave the Pennsylvania Station at a quarter to four . . .*

"Don't you just *loathe* this song, Gloria?" a man asks me in a tone of voice so distinct I'm sure we've spoken before. I turn around, holding my martini sociably close to my mouth. I smile and somehow I'm smiling at Art Reingold. Art looks only slightly more formal than he did at Chat. "I thought I might find you at the bar."

I glance down at my clothes. In the past couple of days I've let my appearance go, since nobody seems to care how I look anymore. The jacket is vintage and on permanent loan from my father, but my shoes are flats and I suspect the soles are synthetic.

"You look fine, Gloria. Like the star editor of a legendary magazine."

I frown. "I wasn't aware that you thought so highly of *Portfolio*."

"I don't."

He tells me that he's reserved a table for us and would I mind joining him there? His hand grazes the small of my back. We walk.

"Have you found an editor for *The Algonquin* yet?" I ask, to be polite. "I suppose you're here on business."

People move aside to let us pass. Most of the women are as colorful with their hair dye as they are with their clothing. Their black-and-white husbands look uncomfortably sober next to these bright birds of prey, and the only way to distinguish them from the waiters is to check for the telltale Rolex.

Art gently guides me to our table, lifts away my seat, and then tucks me in. "I *am* on business of sorts," he says. "Isn't everything? I hope you won't object to my selection." Before us on the table is in miniature everything at the buffet: a smorgasbord of calamari and prosciutto and roasted vegetables and cheese and fruit. There's also a plate of baked hors d'oeuvres, cooked in such a way as to render them unidentifiable. They look like remnants from a Civil War battlefield, and I expect to see museum acquisition numbers somewhere on their undersides. I sip my martini. Art does as I do. His lips barely touch the rim of the glass.

"You look surprised to see me, Gloria."

"I didn't realize you were such a patron of the Absinthe Club." I smile. "I'm sure you've heard about the Pulitzer. I tried to call you."

"I tried to call *you*. Your receptionist said you were taking some time off."

The band starts playing "Don't Sit Under the Apple Tree." Our food remains undisturbed. A waiter, or perhaps a bored society husband, has brought me another martini. When I finish, I ask Art to the dance floor.

"I don't dance."

"Then I'll waltz by myself."

We stand. Two or three other couples are already on the floor, gently swaying in place like sinking ships. I lead. I begin with a slow box step, then graduate into a fox trot.

"To answer your question, Gloria, I still don't have an editor," Art says, speaking into my shoulder. "Right now, I'm waiting for a yes."

"I can see how it might be difficult," I respond. We weave between the other couples. As we pass, the women glare at me, their grips tightening on their husbands. "The Pulitzer Committee has trouble with the word, too."

"The prize was an important test."

"I think I might resign from *Portfolio*."

"It's the graceful thing to do."

"I knew you'd understand."

I quicken the pace. The gin pleasantly cradles my body and numbs my thoughts.

"You'll go immediately, I suppose."

"I think I might leave the country."

"What would you do abroad? Is there an offer?" We dip, then twist. "I shouldn't have done this to you, Gloria. I should have reached a decision before the Pulitzer. Everything was so obvious."

"Isn't it always?"

"What is it you want, Gloria?" Art pulls away briefly so he can look at me, into my eyes. "I know you didn't deserve to win and you know it, too, but you understand that the off chance was always there. Pulitzers are for newspapers, and the last thing I want to associate *The Algonquin* with is newsprint. Surely you can imagine how a Pulitzer-winning editor would hurt morale. What would happen to all the delightful controversy you've cultivated? We'd have to start over, and that might put you in prison. I couldn't have some common prize associated with my magazine, Gloria. You understand image. The value of a good story. Our image has to be protected."

The song has ended. A pear-shaped man in a white double-breasted jacket has taken the microphone and is thanking everyone for coming. It's Bobby Gonzalez, owner of the Absinthe Club as well as fifteen of the city's largest Laundromats. He says the band will be taking a short break, but will be back at the snap of his fingers.

"So now you're after a yes." I'm still holding one of Art's icy hands. I let it go. We've reached the end. The logical conclusion, which should have been obvious from the day I started at *Portfolio*. I will edit *The Algonquin*.

"It's something I have to think about," I tell him.

SEVEN

I CAN'T BELIEVE YOU <u>LIED</u> TO US, GLORIA," Deirdre whines. "That's all I'm saying." We're at Excess Baggage in the San Francisco Shopping Center. It's Saturday. We're looking for a briefcase. I've decided not to take my old one to New York with me.

"This is fucking ridiculous. Why do they assume that because we're women we want our briefcases to resemble overstuffed pillows?" I poke at one, light brown and as soft as water. My finger leaves a dent in its skinlike surface.

"You're not answering my question, Glor."

"Maybe I'm a little bit pathological."

"It's not even the lying. We're used to that. But you know the only reason I moved here is because of you and your fucking magazine. I think you're being unfair."

"*I'm* being unfair. If you want real injustice, look around you. This is a fucking luggage store, and here's the best they can do: pretend bags for pretend businesswomen. Bags as soft as we are. Bags cosmetically suited to us."

"We could try Macy's," Deirdre suggests, briefly abandoning her crusade to establish my fundamental dishonesty.

"It's insulting. Demeaning, really. Do you know the way there?"

She leads me through the door and into the marble atrium. "So, are you still screwing the Russian?" she asks, to change the subject.

"The Russian? He's illiterate. I *am* screwing him, but I doubt he'll appreciate it."

"Making him double up on condoms again?"

We pass a newsstand. "I forgot," I sigh. "You're illiterate, too." From the top rack, I lift the new issue of *The Algonquin*, with its faux-Impressionist cover of flowers abloom and toy sailboats afloat in Central Park.

"But you haven't started."

"Read." I thumb to page forty-seven. "Special arrangements were made in my contract."

PUBLISH OR PERISH

Did Portfolio *fabricate evidence to make its case against the Federal Bureau of Investigation? Gloria Greene, former editor-in-chief, reveals the depths to which one ruthless publisher went—and the careers he destroyed—to save a sinking magazine.*

"But you assigned the cover story. You edited it."

"Dmitri wanted credit. I'm giving him credit."

"*Conscientious resignation?*" She's skimming still. "You were offered a better job. After you were effectively fired."

"That doesn't give the media the right to grossly distort fact for its own gain. The FBI knew Perry Nash was innocent. Yet Dmitri's magazine manipulated Georgia's article to suppress that information, or rather to make it look like the FBI was trying to hide the facts. Why do you think the issue was printed so quickly?"

"You really expect people to believe this?" She wags the magazine at me. Already we're thirty feet from the newsstand. Walking into a camping supply store to escape an angry unpaid newsstand employee.

"Yes. I do." I lower my voice to fit the space. "People forget details. What they remember are stories. Mine is the most compelling tale. As the accused, I am the victim. Victims are untouchable. Surely you understand the investigation will go nowhere. If you were the FBI, would you put your lone ally in jail? Discredit your own witness?"

"I will never understand you, Glor." Deirdre pockets iodine tablets. One bottle of each brand, probably for a taste test or something. I open a bottle. Swallow two tablets. "You also said you got along with Brody and Emmett. You said they were in love with you, Glor, and that didn't stop them from trying to throw you in jail. You are suspected of first-degree murder. Of killing an innocent man, your boss, so you could take his job. The FBI isn't going to forget about you because you did them some small favor . . . that cost you nothing."

"*Some small favor? That cost me nothing?* This is my life, Deirdre. I've spent every moment working my way up to a position where that *small favor* was even within the realm of possibility. Those assholes had fucking better appreciate it."

"And if they don't?"

"As I already explained, they'll do more damage to themselves than they can ever inflict on me if they arrest me without concrete evidence. This case is too public for comfort."

"Do you think they'll ever find out who did it?"

"Perfect crimes are boring, Deir. They're perfectly forgettable. Everybody involved wants them to just go away." I smile. "But unless I find a decent briefcase, I'm never going to survive Manhattan."

"You're impossible, Glor. Are you sure I won't have to visit you in jail? When are we going to lunch? I thought you already *found* a briefcase with your father."

"That's what I intended, but Daddy's been too irate about my move, and he won't look with me. It's like I'm divorcing him or something." I poke at the side of a tent with my foot. "Now that Madison's dumped him for Dmitri, he's threatening to come to New York, too. To keep tabs on me. He's worried about the FBI thing, too. He says I'm dangerous."

"He just can't let go." Deirdre disappears behind a display of canteens and mess kits and mysterious configurations of brightly tinted aluminum that must have something to do with suspension of disbelief. "How about a commuter kayak instead?" She giggles. "Or . . . an attaché for the urban jungle?"

Deirdre emerges with a pith helmet on her head and a hunting satchel slung across her shoulder. The buckles work, and it's made of leather that smells of horses and of brass that sounds of firmly clutched hands.

"Can we go now? I'm hungry."

I turn it upside down. I shake it and I can find nothing wrong, no matter what I do.

As usual, Deirdre offers to shoplift it for me. She's eager to do so because she can fill it with things she wants for herself. I tell her she should be more respectful of other people's property. While she pouts, I sign on my credit card.

"Are you really Gloria Greene?" The clerks gather to see. "*The* Gloria Greene?"

On the street, Deirdre takes the bag from me. "This will just be a moment," she promises.

From a hidden compartment deep inside the bag she withdraws an object wrapped in parachute cloth. A gift. A survival knife, all bright and silver and sharp as wit. She grins and draws the flat edge across my neck. "In case your career ever stalls in New York . . ."

But of course she isn't serious.